Jeffries

AN ARTFUL DEATH

When expat Keith Vickers's boat is found empty
and drifting out at sea, no one is too worried. But
then Inspector Alvarez discovers that no one has
seen the man for several days . . . so when his body
turns up it isn't exactly a surprise to Alvarez that
the case is now one of murder.

Interviewing the dead man's servants, Alvarez
gets the impression of a notorious philanderer –
a man whose love life is so complicated even
Vickers himself probably had trouble remembering
its intricacies. And one of those intricacies is British
cabinet minister George Lovell, a man staying
on Mallorca with his cousin; a man who was
overheard arguing with Vickers on the day of his
disappearance.

As Alvarez continues his investigation, he makes
his suspicions of Lovell rather too obvious, with
the inevitable result that an official complaint is
lodged. So once more he finds himself the target
of Superior Chief Salas's vitriolic tongue. And as if
that were not enough, he still has a case to solve.

A delightful and witty mystery featuring Roderic
Jeffries's much-loved Inspector Alvarez.

AN ARTFUL DEATH

AN INSPECTOR ALVAREZ NOVEL

Roderic Jeffries

HarperCollins*Publishers*

This novel is entirely a work of fiction. The names,
characters and incidents portrayed in it are the work of the
author's imagination. Any resemblance to actual persons,
living or dead, events or localities is entirely coincidental.

Collins Crime
An imprint of HarperCollins*Publishers*
77–85 Fulham Palace Road, London W6 8JB

The Collins Crime website address is:
www.fireandwater.com/crime

First published in Great Britain
in 2000 by Collins Crime

1 3 5 7 9 10 8 6 4 2

A catalogue record for this book
is available from the British Library

ISBN 0 00 232703 1

Set in Meridien and Bodoni by
Palimpsest Book Production Limited,
Polmont, Stirlingshire

Printed and bound in Great Britain by
Clays Ltd, St Ives plc

AN ARTFUL DEATH

CHAPTER 1

Orange, lemon, tangerine and grapefruit trees curled their leaves; animals in the fields sought any patch of shade to be found; birds did not fly; shutters were kept closed; tourists lay on the beaches and fried, to the profit of local doctors. It was the hottest day of the year.

Dale stepped out of the air-conditioned sitting room on to the covered patio, beyond which was a swimming pool, backed by a small lawn.

'Who rang?' Geraldine asked.

He sat, picked up his glass from the table. 'George.'

'Did you remember to ask how Angela is – her operation was yesterday?'

'Regretfully, not her George. It was Cousin George, recently seen trying out nimbuses for size.'

'What on earth did he want?'

'To do us the honour of staying here for a few days next week.'

'I hope you told him we were off to Timbuktu tonight?'

'You underrate his duplicity. He began by wondering if we were returning to the UK in the near future. Fearing he was about to ask some impossible favour, I said very firmly that we weren't thinking of doing that until the weather changed which wouldn't be for weeks. At which point, he trumped my ace. If we were going to be here, he knew we'd be delighted to have him stay . . . Isn't it interesting how politicians can easily believe the impossible, whereas the possible always defeats them?'

'Maybe he won't be able to get a flight. Madge was telling me that friends of theirs have been trying to come out for days, but airlines are booked right up.'

1

'He'll marshal every ounce of influence.'

'If only he weren't so aggressively arrogant.'

'A perfect cloak for ignorance.'

'Is Helen coming with him?'

'He said not. Hardly surprising she should seize the chance of a short apartness – I've always maintained that even though she married him, basically she's an intelligent woman.' He drained his glass, stood. 'How about a refill?'

'A very large one . . . Who was it wrote that God provides our relatives but thankfully leaves the choice of friends to us?'

'Someone who has a Cousin George.'

He picked up the two glasses and crossed the patio to the house, went inside. Having a broad sense of humour (Geraldine sometimes called it twisted) the coming visit did not disturb him as much as it did her. There was much ironic amusement to be gained from listening to George pontificate.

Cellars were unusual, but Ca Na Atalla had one because when it was being built, the man operating the earth-moving machine had, typically, not bothered with the plans and had dug far too large a hole for the cisterna. It had been a happy mistake; even a few metres down, the temperature was noticeably cooler. He poured out two generous gin and tonics, carried the glasses out to the patio, sat. 'Remind me to check the level of the water and see if we need to order another lorryload.'

'Do it now, whilst you remember.'

'Watch your language, woman. On this island, "now" is a three-letter word.'

She drank. 'The only other time George was here, he itemized everything that was wrong with the place. If he dislikes it so much, why doesn't he go to somewhere exotic where there's a chance of his being kidnapped and held to ransom? I'm sure the government would be happy to refuse to pay.'

'He wants to see us.'

'Didn't you explain that the feeling isn't mutual?'

'Come on, Gerry, he's not really that awful.'

'I'll remind you of that when you come fuming into the kitchen to tell me that if he doesn't stop talking cock-eyed politics, you'll do him a serious injury.'

'Just look on the bright side of things.'

'Such a fatuous comment has to be a cry of despair!'

'On the contrary, a call for the return to Victorian values . . . There was one thing a little odd about the conversation. He asked if Keith Vickers was here; asked so very casually I got the impression he wanted to make certain Keith was before he booked in with us.'

'That doesn't sound very likely. There's never been any suggestion they're friends. In fact, I don't know for certain they've ever met.'

'True. But think on this. As you said, Mallorca just isn't his scene. The butcher, the baker and the candlestick maker holiday here, so members of the government keep well away – their doctrine of equality must never be exaggerated. So why did he ever come here in the first place? Remember last time he asked if he could borrow one of our cars to drive to see someone? When I gave him the keys and showed him the controls of the Citroën, I casually asked who he was meeting? He curtly said I wouldn't know the person and left it at that. Now, I'm wondering if it was Keith.'

'That really would be a case of chalk and cheese.'

'More chalk and cheesy . . . Or could we have been misjudging George all these years? Perhaps he's not the withered prune he appears to be and beneath that mask there beats an ocean of Rabelaisian desires and he's hoping that under Keith's tutelage he'll fulfil at least some of these.'

'You're mixing up your mind with his.'

CHAPTER 2

Ca'n Mortice had been built for a Frenchman who had gained permission to sidestep planning restrictions by the many subtleties to be found in a brown envelope. It stood roughly halfway along the Parelona Peninsula, on the north side of a small, east-facing cove; from it, there was an uninterrupted, if limited, view to the distant horizon. There was not another building within many kilometres, but because electricity had been taken across the mountains and hills to the lighthouse at the tip of the peninsula, it had been possible to connect power to the house. It had its own water supply – a well which, confusingly, had been sunk halfway up the hill that backed the house and appeared to pose the question, could water flow uphill? Because the cove shelved steeply, there was good mooring for even a large boat and a concrete landing stage stretched out into the water. There were no private beaches in Spain, but access to any beach was not an inalienable right; since all the land back to the road was owned, only those who arrived by boat could enjoy the crystal-clear water and pebble beach. To ensure their number was very small, a notice in Spanish, German, French and English was posted on each bank, which falsely declared the cove to be government property and forbidden to unauthorized persons.

Such beautiful solitude provoked images of an idyllic life. Yet the Frenchman died from a heart attack just over a year after moving into the house; whilst his companion suffered embarrassment from the circumstances of his death, this was overtaken when she learned that he had left his fortune to his family whom he'd deserted several years before. The French, she would tell anyone who would listen, didn't know the meaning of loyalty.

Estate agents thought the property would be difficult to sell; and its location was a major drawback since to reach the nearest shop, one had either to sail round to Port Llueso or drive on the twisting, turning, largely unguarded mountain road, made even more dangerous by Spaniards who ignored central lines and Germans who were seldom aware there were any. The estate agents were proved wrong. Four months after first coming on the market, Keith Vickers bought Ca'n Mortice, attracted by the setting, but also by the fact that obviously only a very wealthy man could afford to live there.

He usually claimed that he had been born into poverty and worked his way into wealth against all the odds, but like so much of his life, this was a lie. His father had been a partner in a solid, country accountancy firm and his home had reflected a comfortable life. He had been to Arborne, a minor public school, from which he had not been expelled after being found in bed in a nearby girls' school because at that time the school had been suffering financial difficulties. This had taught him that a conflict between morals and money was a no-contest.

After gaining a poor degree – and an allegation of fatherhood – at a second-rate university, his father, a cautious man, had suggested he join an accountancy firm other than his own. For many months, the work had proved so boring that Vickers would have thrown in his hand had he not been pursuing one of the secretaries who was proving unaccountably resistant to his priapic charms, but then his eyes were opened. Part of a team investigating the affairs of a once prosperous firm brought to the point of bankruptcy by the financial chicanery of the managing director, he had realized that had the managing director truly appreciated and understood the magic of figures – mathematical ones, that was – he would have enriched himself even more at other people's expense and that without being exposed. Vickers had discovered the secret charm of accountancy. From then on, he had worked with a dedication that had surprised his seniors.

When satisfied he'd learned all that was necessary, he had left the firm – to his father's consternation, but then he was conservative and aging – and set up on his own. From there it had not been too great a step to move into property and property development. Shortly before his death, his father, worried about certain rumours he had heard, had reminded him of the moral standards of his professional calling; he'd assured his father that he never had, and never would, pursue an immoral profit and had been amused when he'd been unreservedly believed. It was the credulity of the honest which would always ensure the financial comfort of those who perceived both honesty and dishonesty as being no more than tools to be used as and when appropriate.

He regarded his marriage as his one major mistake and could never satisfy himself as to why he had made it.

He walked round the large swimming pool and into the pool complex, crossed to the refrigerator and brought out a bottle of Veuve Clicquot which he dropped into an insulated container. Few of his fellow expatriates drank champagne because it was more than three times as expensive as a good cava; it amused him when they claimed they drank cava because it was just as good and not because of the price. Not that, blindfolded, he could have told the difference.

He sat at one of the three round patio tables set within the shade, filled his glass, and stared out at the cove as he drank. It was a sight that gave him great satisfaction because he owned the rocks which plunged into the postcard-blue water and the pine trees which somehow found life on their steep surfaces; the sixty-nine-foot motor cruiser, moored to the jetty, a larger boat than any of the local expatriates owned; the valley, not visible from where he sat . . .

Movement disturbed his thoughts. A large bird planed across the bay, its wings widespread. An osprey, an Eleonora's falcon? One of his women – for the moment, he couldn't remember which – had been an avid bird-watcher and she would instantly have identified it. It had amused him that anyone should become so interested in something incapable of showing profit . . .

He heard a distant sound and turned to look up the slope at the house. Rosa walked down towards him. Short,

7

stocky, she was a typical local in her middle forties. The Mediterranean produced considerable beauty, but it was usually short-lived, whether human, floral, or scenic – the last, thanks to tourism.

'Señor, there is a call, but it is not working.' She held out a cordless phone.

Because her English was about on a par with his Spanish, it took him a moment to work out the fact that it was the phone in the pool house which, yet again, was not working – only two days before, he'd had it repaired and had been assured by the technician that all was now well. The locals were good at assurances. He took the receiver from Rosa and as she returned up the slope to the house, he answered the call.

'It's Teddy here.'

'Good to hear from you.'

'What's the weather like?'

'Cloudless and boiling hot.'

'Some people have all the luck!'

One made one's own luck. Ryder was too conservative ever to become lucky. But he was loyal, intelligent, and had an accommodating conscience, which made him a good man to have in charge of the actual running of the companies – if he fiddled, which it was to be presumed he did, it would never be to the extent that he might easily be found out. The person who was content with small illegal profits was a valuable employee. 'Is anything new?'

'The wink's just come through that we will gain planning permission for the new development. That's great, isn't it?'

'Sure.' Having spent a small fortune on smoothing paths, he had expected nothing less.

It was a long telephone call. Ryder liked to dot every i and cross every t; no point was too small to be ignored. But that suited Vickers because it meant he could be in full control of everything even though he spent most of the year on the island.

Having said goodbye, he switched off the phone and laid it down on the table. He stared out at the cove once again.

Assuming the development went ahead, he would become even wealthier. Money was the key which opened every lock. Here, on the island, there were still expatriates who thought background and manners counted for more than wealth. That was why they drank cava. He refilled his glass with champagne.

He thought about Melanie. A redhead with looks that couldn't readily be classified. She wasn't beautiful in either classical or catwalk sense; her features were irregular; she had a shapely body, but didn't bother to make the best of it and often wore clothes that could hardly have been less soignée, but the whole was very much greater than the parts. She immediately made a man think of a king-sized bed because that would afford great freedom of movement. Which made it all the more infuriating that she continued to rebuff his attempts to turn thoughts into reality . . . Yet perhaps he was making better progress than might seem apparent. When he'd casually suggested it might be fun to sail over to Monte Carlo for a day or two and have a flutter at the tables, she hadn't immediately laughed a rejection . . .

The phone rang. He picked it up, switched it on, extended the aerial, answered the call.

'It's Serena.'

When he remembered who she was, he silently swore. Some women lacked even enough sense to understand that a past affair was buried history.

'Are you still there?'

'Yes.'

'I'm in Alassio. That's in Italy . . .'

'Forget the geography lesson.'

'I . . . I need help, Keith.'

'Really.'

'For God's sake, don't be like that.'

'Perhaps you've forgotten what I said – *finito*.'

'I know, but . . .'

He pictured her face, now so contorted by worry and fear that she lost her looks which were her only asset. There was a soft streak in her which earned his contempt.

'I owe the landlord two months' rent and he says that if I don't pay up inside a week, he'll have me thrown out. Keith, I'm bloody scared. I've nowhere else to go. What can I do?'

'Stay with friends.'

'I haven't got any here.'

He shrugged his shoulders, lifted the glass. As he drank, he decided that the man who'd said only sex beat champagne on a hot day knew what he was talking about.

'I'm real skint, Keith.'

'What's happened to all I gave you?'

'That was a long time ago and it wasn't all that much.'

'It would have been had you been careful.'

'It wasn't my fault. Grant swore he would –'

'Who?'

'A bloke from Cardiff I met. He told me he'd a really good job waiting for him in Alassio, so that's why we came here. And he said we'd have a nice flat, even though it would cost, because he'd pay for it . . . The job wasn't there. And he pinched all my cash and just vanished. Keith, I'm scared. I gave up my job as a courier to be with you and that firm won't ever take anyone back however good you've been. I've tried all the British firms operating here, but it's the wrong time of the season and the only one who might have had a job going wanted fluent Italian, so my Spanish is useless. I've been round all the shops, I've tried everything. I'm going to be flung out of the flat . . .'

'Go back to your family.'

'After Mum died, Dad took up with a real bitch and she hates me. I've told you that before. Give me enough to pay off the landlord and live until I find a job; please, please.'

'You've just said there aren't any jobs.'

'Something's bound to turn up if only I can hang on.'

'Look, kid, some good advice. That's the kind of thinking that can only lead to more trouble.'

'But I'm certain it's true. Just lend me the money. I swear I'll repay it.'

'I never lend money because it spoils a relationship.'

Once she appreciated the cruel irony of that remark, she began to cry.

He cut the connection. There was not much he disliked more than a weeping woman. He drank and he thought that there was the odd occasion when champagne was the greater pleasure.

CHAPTER 3

Mrs Foster had lived longer in the area than all but one of the British expatriates. Her husband and she had designed the large house, and, despite the best attempts of the architect, aparejador, and builder, had managed to imbue it with taste. Considerable use had been made of traditional Spanish designs, especially in regard to the panelled doors. The garden was a pleasing mixture of Mediterranean slapdash and English informal and there was colour throughout every month. For more than twenty years, the gardener had been trying to persuade her to let him dig up several of the flower beds and much of the lawn and replant with vegetables which would be of some use.

When her husband had died, she had with the stoic determination of her generation, given small indication of the bitter sense of loss she felt; in consequence there were many who considered her cold and unfeeling.

For no readily discernible reason, cocktail parties had gone out of fashion, much to the regret of those who liked to drink at the expense of others, but she continued to give lavish ones to which she invited everyone she knew – which meant those she cared to know, because she did not bend to fashion and saw no reason to equate wealth with breeding. She could be called a snob, but her judgements were based on different standards from modern ones and within that remit she was not a snob.

The fifty guests were mainly grouped around the oval pool. Two maids carried around plates of canapés and the butler, husband of one of the maids, made certain that no glass unwillingly remained empty. Those who criticized Mrs Foster for her character, had to concede that her hospitality was beyond question.

Lovell, standing by the steps into the pool, had gathered around him a small group of listeners; not only did he appear frequently on television, when on an imaginary soapbox he could project an air of warm concern for the good of the human race.

Geraldine, Dale and Pilcher found themselves closer to Lovell than they would have wished.

'Doesn't he realize he's meant to be on holiday?' Pilcher asked, as Lovell mentioned the Prime Minister and himself in the same sentence for the third time in as many minutes.

'Unfortunately, no,' Dale answered. 'Over breakfast this morning, we were subjected to a lecture on agriculture in Barbados.'

'What does he know about that?'

'Everything possible, since recently he's been on a two-day parliamentary visit to the island.'

'What was the point?'

'England was having lousy weather.'

'Half the money the government steals in taxes goes to filling the troughs that he and his ilk gorge from.'

'Should that worry you? Surely you don't pay any taxes?'

'Of course not.'

'It's the principle of the thing that sticks in your gullet?' Geraldine sweetly suggested.

'I say, Esme, what have you been doing to my favourite lady to make her as sharp as she is tonight?' Pilcher asked lightly.

'Nothing of which I'm aware,' Dale replied. 'But then she'll tell you that no husband is ever sufficiently emotionally responsive to know if he's upsetting his wife.'

The butler came up to where they stood. 'Champagne, señors?'

They held out their glasses which were topped up from the bottle of Mumm.

As the butler walked away, she said: 'Typical Spanish male chauvinism!'

The two men looked at each other.

'And your reaction to that is even more typical! Neither of

14

you began to realize he said señors, not señora and señors. In this country, women are treated like second-class citizens.'

'Which is why it's such a pleasure to live here,' Pilcher said.

'For that remark, I withdraw the invitation to lunch. Susan will be welcome, you won't.'

'She'll never leave me behind.'

'She'll jump at the chance.'

'On which note, I'll gracefully depart on the grounds that I have to deliver Susan from the verbal arms of whichever of the many bores here has waylaid her.'

They watched him leave, threading his way between people. 'You sounded a bit cutting,' Dale observed.

'Good! He ought to have matured sufficiently not to make that sort of stupid remark ... And don't you add your halfpenny worth or I'll kick you where it really hurts.'

'In the face of such a threat, I've nothing to say ... Don't you think it's time to make a move?'

'Yes. But you'll have to extract George.'

Dale looked to his right. 'He's still in full stream. I wonder where he gets it from, since, according to family tradition, his father was the most taciturn of men.'

'I suppose now you're about to blame his mother's genes?'

'I wouldn't dare.'

'Make signs at him to say it's time to go.'

'Is that wise? He'll probably think we're applauding him.'

Mrs Foster walked up to them. 'I've been trying all evening to have a word with you. Look, you're to stay for a light supper.'

'That would be great, but you can't possibly want us around any longer with all the clearing up there'll be,' Geraldine answered.

'It's only a little cold meat and salad. Do stay. It's such a pleasure to have an intelligent conversation after all the inane waffle.'

'I'm afraid it would mean your having Esme's cousin, George, as well.'

Dale said: 'And that would involve more inane waffle

in the first five minutes than you've heard all evening so far.'

'The pleasure of having you two will make up for that. Do stay on.'

'Then we'd love to,' Geraldine said. 'And why not put George next to Esme at the far end of the table?'

'Why suggest that?' Dale protested.

'To teach you not to agree with Andrew when he makes one of his silly remarks.'

'I never said a thing.'

'Precisely.'

The master bedroom, with an *en suite* bathroom and small changing room, was on the top floor of Ca Na Atalla. From this there was a view to the west of the mountains which marked the southern end of the Laraix valley, to the north, no more than half a kilometre away, were hills which soon rose to become mountains.

Geraldine switched off the air-conditioning unit, climbed into the left-hand bed (because of the heat, separate beds were a common feature for married couples). She did not lie down, but remained sitting up. 'I suppose . . .' She stopped.

'What?' Dale asked, as he pulled on a pair of pyjama trousers. Bare-chested, he climbed into the right-hand bed.

'Nothing.'

'Which in female language means something of great importance.'

'If you must know, I'm curious when I shouldn't be.'

'A common female complaint.'

'That's not even funny. George wanted to make a phone call when we got back here, didn't he? Did he ask you what the new code for International is?'

'No.'

'Then he can't have dialled it. And if he'd tried the old code, he'd have been told in Spanish what he was doing wrong and he wouldn't have understood a word and would have come complaining to us that the Spanish phone people speak their own language instead of his.'

'More than likely.'

'So it must have been a local call. Who's he going to phone at midnight?'

'Do I get a kiss for telling you?'

'It's too hot.'

'I can turn the air-conditioning back on.'

'There are times when I agree with Madge.'

'She changes her mind so often, I'd have thought that an impossibility.'

'Her opinion of men is fixed.'

'Because she's a frustrated woman.'

'You made an approach, but were rejected? Poor man!'

'There must be more unlikely events, but I can't think what they can be . . . So do you want to know who Cousin George was phoning?'

'No.' She began to read. After a moment, she said: 'Who?'

'Keith.'

'How do you know?'

'I chanced to be within earshot.'

'Chanced?'

'And naturally at the first opportunity hurriedly removed myself out of earshot.'

'The perfect gentleman – once you've got what you want . . . Are you saying it was Keith Vickers?'

'Can you name another Keith?'

'No. But then there are any number of new residents we don't know and he could be a tourist.'

'Remember how, when he phoned to say he wanted to come here for a few days, he so very casually asked if Keith Vickers was on the island?'

'But why? How can they have anything in common, especially that late at night?'

'Women?'

'I thought you'd say that.'

'I have another suggestion.'

'Men?'

'George is hoping Keith will make a very generous contribution to party funds and is buttering him up.'

'Keith would want something very solid in return.'

'So George dangles the standard political bait for the nouveau riche – a title.'

'My God!'

'The mind does boggle, but in fact these days most titles end up with those least able to carry them with the necessary style and prideful humility.'

'I don't know whether to laugh or cry at the thought of Lord Vickers.'

'If you're about to cry, I'll come into your bed and comfort you.'

'I must remember to make certain you don't drink so much champagne another time.'

CHAPTER 4

Occasionally a man could enjoy life without the fear that he was about to fall over, break a bone, and whilst in hospital contract an infection that proved resistant to antibiotics and therefore fatal. Alvarez slumped back in the chair and closed his eyes the better to appreciate the pleasure of the moment. Superior Chief Salas was in Salamanca, attending a conference, and on the morning news it had been announced that Salamanca was suffering a flu epidemic which was causing the medical profession considerable worry because the strain was severe and an outbreak at such a time of the year was unusual. Even ordinary flu was highly contagious . . . Dolores was in one of her good moods and this guaranteed that lunch would be a Lucullan feast . . .

When he awoke, it was almost one o'clock and he congratulated himself on an interior alarm that roused him to leave the office on time. He yawned, suddenly remembered Dolores had asked him to buy something on the way home. But what? Small matter. Whatever it was she wanted, she could go out and get it when she had a spare moment.

He left the office, went down the stairs and along the corridor, past a morose-looking duty cabo, and out into the street. He crossed the road to reach the shade, automatically began to walk towards the old square where his car was normally parked, and abruptly came to a stop. Due to some inexplicable reason, and no doubt a large Euro grant, the square had been dug up. He silently swore as he turned and began the long trudge to where his car was now parked. The doctor said he was out of condition because he ate, drank and smoked too much and lacked exercise, but doctors seemed to equate physical health with suffering.

He reached his Ibiza, unlocked the driving door, settled behind the wheel, started the engine, and drove off. When almost home, he remembered what it was that Dolores had told him to bring – wine. There might not be enough in the house for the coming meal. He turned down a side road, parked in front of the only general store in the village which had not succumbed to modernity. More like a barn than a shop, the long triangular ceiling was bare and the walls were unpainted. Goods were stacked in rows on the floor in individual piles and no attempt had been made to position like with like; having bought a tin of baked beans, one might well have to search hard and long to find a tin of red beans. Only the wine was carefully together, in the cardboard cases in which it had been delivered. An ignorant foreigner might well assume that in such a primitive store, only vino corriente would be sold, but the owner was an oenophile and some of the finest Spanish wines were on offer – which, as every Spaniard knew, were at least the equal of, and often superior to, overrated French ones. He walked up and down the line of boxes, mentally savouring the wines they contained and wondering how extravagant he would let himself be. In the end, he bought three bottles of Marqués de Cáceres.

Juan and Isabel were playing with friends in the street outside their home, and while the girl greeted him as he stepped out on to the road, Juan did not. How times had changed, he thought sadly; in his day a boy of Juan's age would never have ignored his uncle – even when in truth the relationship was more remote than that. Family ties were breaking down; youth no longer had respect for age; principles were jeered at; standards were ignored . . . He picked up the wine in a plastic bag and felt more cheerful. Perhaps things weren't as they had been, but in most cases that was cause for rejoicing. Fifty years ago, the thought of an inspector in the Cuerpo being able to afford to buy three bottles of good Rioja would have been absurd . . .

He entered the house, went through the front room that was kept so clean dust particles felt lonely, and into the sitting/dining room. Jaime sat on the far side of the table, a glass, a bottle of Soberano, and an insulated ice container in front of him. From the kitchen came the sound of singing.

Alvarez looked at the bead curtain, spoke quietly: 'She's still in a good mood, then. Have you any idea what's for lunch?'

'How would I know?'

'You might have gained an idea?'

'I haven't . . . Have you got the wine?'

He put the bag on the table.

'I told her she'd better get out and buy some because you'd never remember, but she said that when it was your stomach at risk, you would . . . What d'you buy?'

He lifted the three bottles out of the bag.

'You're doing us proud!'

Alvarez sat, reached over to the sideboard and from it brought a glass. He poured himself a generous brandy, added three ice cubes.

Dolores pushed her way through the bead curtain. She was sweating, her hair was slightly dishevelled, and the apron she wore had recently been stained, but her face was lined with proud authority and had she worn traditional dress on her still shapely body, she might have been an Andaluce about to mount her caparisoned horse to ride past admiring crowds. 'I see you're drinking.'

They looked at each other.

'Would you like another few minutes before I dish?'

'Might as well,' Jaime mumbled, confused by such uncritical thoughtfulness.

'Another ten minutes, then. And will one of you call the kids in?'

She returned through the bead curtain into the kitchen. Alvarez drank, put the glass down on the table, leaned forward. 'You must have done something that really pleased her; so what was it?'

'I've said, I don't know. Wouldn't I keep doing it if I did?'

Alvarez sighed. 'Sure. But the world being what it is, maybe

it would cease having an effect. Eat lamb every day for a month and yesterday's chickpeas can taste good.'

'What's lamb and chickpeas to do with it?'

Alvarez drank, offered Jaime a cigarette, and lit a match for both of them, at which point he remembered the doctor's warning – when it was too late. He poured himself another brandy.

Dolores looked through the bead curtain. 'Are you ready now?'

Jaime nodded.

'Have you called the children?' When there was no answer, she said: 'Sometimes I wonder why men still have legs since it's the women who have to do all the running.' But her tone had been light and as she passed through to the front room, she was smiling.

'It's days since she last yelled at me,' Jaime said. 'Maybe she's learning how to be a proper wife.'

'If the sheep are lambing without trouble, don't think that tomorrow they won't be aborting.'

Jaime drank. 'Sometimes,' he said, as he wiped his mouth with the back of his hand, 'I just don't understand what you're on about.'

Alvarez lay on his bed and assured himself he had divined the secret of happiness. Then, infuriatingly, he remembered warning Jaime that to enjoy a pleasure too frequently was to render it a pleasure no longer. Why was man condemned to be unable to live as did the gods? Had they, with the hypocrisy of the rich praising the value of honesty above wealth, decided man must never be allowed to enjoy himself for long? Perhaps, but the will of the gods could be delayed, if not defeated. There was one bottle of Marqués de Cáceres left unopened, another could be purchased, and Salas would not be back tomorrow. Only one other element was essential. Dolores must retain her present mood. Could even the gods determine that?

CHAPTER 5

As Rosa listened to Luisa's ecstatic, jumbled description of the previous evening when she and Ricardo had decided to marry as soon as it became financially feasible, she wondered how long their days would remain golden. Not for ever was the only certainty. When her Pedro had proposed, she'd felt as if a rainbow had sheathed her, but it hadn't been long before only the rain remained. Pedro had always considered himself first, had disliked work but liked bars, and only months after their marriage, gossip had said he was very often on the beaches with young foreign women who wore such little clothing that a decent woman had to look away . . . Yet, so illogical was human emotion, she had felt as if part of her had been scooped out with a red-hot knife when he'd died . . .

'He has an aunt with two fincas and she'll give us one of 'em. Of course, it's not in a good state, but he'll spend every evening after work reforming it completely. There's a good well and the electricity goes to the next house so there won't be any trouble in getting connected. We've decided which will be our bedroom . . .'

'Make certain he doesn't suggest you try it out before you're married.'

'He's not like that. He's said, there won't be anything before we're married.'

Rosa sighed. Women suffered many burdens and one of the heaviest was the fact that each of them had to learn the truth for herself.

'And furnishing's easy. My Aunt Teresa has that shop near the Remembrance Gardens and she'll let us have what we want at cost price. Then there's Cousin Natalia in Inca who sells fabrics and although she's a bit of a tightwad, she'll probably give us bed linen cheaply . . .'

Rosa ceased to listen as she pondered life. Her parents had married, returned to work the same afternoon, and lived in a one-bedroom caseta furnished with only the bare necessities; when she and Pedro had been married, their flat had been small, but it had had two bedrooms and they had been able to afford what had then been a great luxury, a refrigerator, which they'd kept in the sitting room so that guests could be witness to their good luck; when Luisa and Ricardo married – assuming she was not so stupid as to let him discover marriage was unnecessary – they would live in a finca, every room would be fully furnished, and the refrigerator would be only one of many pieces of electrical equipment in the kitchen. Yet in truth, she didn't begrudge them their good fortune – that was, provided they didn't waste it with the stupidity of which the young seemed so capable . . . She looked up at the electric clock on the far wall. 'You'd better find out if the señor's ready for breakfast and does he want anything cooked? Oh, and tell him there was a phone call last night from Señorita Lockwood.'

'What did she want?'

'That's her business.'

'Only asking.'

'As a matter of fact, she said, did I know where he'd got to?'

'So what did you answer?'

'That I'd no idea . . . Go and find out about breakfast.'

'I'm not entering the bedroom when he's in bed.'

'Knock and call out.'

'And if he doesn't answer?'

'Put your head round the door. He'll be too sleepy to do anything more than just answer.' Luisa, Rosa thought, had no cause to worry. She might enjoy the sparkle of youth, but her hair was straight and lanky, her face too long, she had a button mouth and a square chin, and it was a kindness to describe her shape as buxom. The señor had the money to amuse himself with women who made every male head turn.

'I'll use the phone.'

'Suit yourself.'

Luisa crossed to the receiver on the wall which could connect with any other in the house or pool complex. She pressed a single number, waited; pressed thrice more, then replaced the receiver. 'He's not in his bedroom, library, television room, or pool house.'

'Then you'd best go down and see if he's still on the boat; maybe he got back so late he couldn't be bothered to come up to the house.' Or . . . When young, she'd secretly, guiltily, read a book on the proscribed list in which one of the characters had taken a girl for a trip on his yacht because until then she had been resisting him all too successfully and, as he knew, the sea did something to a woman. She'd often wondered if there was any truth in that – when the señor had taken them for a trip, she'd suffered no overwhelming desires; but she was not young . . .

As Luisa left the kitchen through the outside door, the bread machine, time-set the previous evening, beeped. Rosa crossed to it, raised the lid and, wearing a kitchen glove, lifted out the inner container and decanted the loaf on to the breadboard. The señor wouldn't eat yesterday's bread, even if that meant wasting half a loaf. It never ceased to astonish her that he seemed incapable of appreciating that to waste anything was to challenge the future. There could come a time when he would sell his soul for half a loaf of stale bread.

Luisa returned. 'Gaspar says the boat's not here.'

'Then he spent the night at sea or tied up somewhere else.'

'So he won't be wanting breakfast.'

'No. You'd best start cleaning –' The telephone interrupted her. She crossed the floor and lifted the receiver. 'Speak.' The señor had tried to persuade her to answer in a manner he claimed to be more polite, but she wasn't going to change the customary response just for him.

'I want to speak to Señor Vickers.'

She recognized the voice. 'He's still not here, Señorita Lockwood.' She found great difficulty in saying 'Lockwood'.

'Of course he is.'

'He is not here.'

'Don't lie.'

Rosa replaced the receiver. She was prepared to put up with many of the foreigners' peculiar habits – in part that was what she was paid to do – but she had too much pride to accept being called a liar.

'Who was that?' Luisa asked.

'That Lockwood woman.'

'Wanting the señor?'

'Who else?'

'If he's not with her, where is he?'

'That's what she really wanted to know . . . You can start in the sitting room.'

'Where's the rush if he's not around?'

'You want to keep this job?'

'Of course I do with me and Ricardo saving hard.'

'Then just remember he's the kind of man who demands value for money.'

'And doesn't care if we work ourselves to death.'

'There's small enough risk of you doing that.'

'Bloody funny!'

'I've told you before about using that kind of language . . .'

'I don't think you even know what century you're in!'

Rosa sighed. The modern young . . .

The phone rang again.

'Rosa, it's Melanie Lockwood again. I'm terribly sorry I spoke as I did, but I'm so worried.'

When the English apologized, you knew they wanted something. 'Señorita?'

'You do understand, don't you, that I didn't mean it?'

Then why say it?

'Will you be kind enough to put me through to Señor Vickers, please?'

Was the woman a complete fool? 'I've told you, señorita, he's not here. His boat's away.'

'Hasn't he phoned to say where he is?'

'No.'

There was a long pause, then: 'But I expect you can guess?'

'No, señorita, I can't.'

'Are you sure? I mean, you're so loyal, maybe you don't want to tell me, but . . .'

Rosa remained silent.

'Look, ask him to phone me the moment he returns home. Say I've been terribly worried because he didn't turn up. Will you do that for me?'

'Yes.'

'I'm really grateful. Goodbye and thank you again. And I do hope he rings me very soon.'

I'll bet, Rosa thought as she replaced the phone. It sounded as if the señorita was worried that she'd played hard-to-get too successfully.

'Was that her again?' Luisa asked.

'Yes.'

'He's found someone else, hasn't he?'

'Seems likely . . . She wants the señor to ring as soon as he comes back.'

'She'll be lucky!'

The Mediterranean had been so over-fished and the potential profits from the tourist trade were so great, that few fishing boats now worked from Port Llueso. However, there were some men, of whom Fiol was one, who because the sea was in their blood or they were too old or proud to learn to work for foreigners, still sailed their locally built boats out into the bay and beyond.

Fiol looked older than his years because his skin was darkened and rippled by the wind, sun and sea, and a lifetime of hard work had bowed his shoulders. Often he had to sail on his own because no one would help him for the money he could afford to pay, but that never bothered him; he welcomed solitude. At sea, when the engine was cut, moving gently and rhythmically amidst a silence broken only by the slap of water against the hull, he felt at one with life and, should that be necessary, death.

When he first saw the motor cruiser, she was halfway to the horizon; he hated all the power boats and yachts which now crowded the waters, had nothing but contempt for the landlubbers who owned them and thought a force-six wind was a hurricane. Half an hour later, he was close enough to be certain she was not under way, that she was over twenty metres in length and – this, a reluctant admission – she was not some over-superstructured gin palace, but a seaworthy-looking craft. He was surprised to see no sign of life. Had all those aboard stupidly gone swimming together? But he could see no one in the water. Then was there some sort of trouble? A seaman always responded to trouble even when that had been provoked by a bloody fool of a foreigner who wasn't fit to handle a dinghy on a lake.

He sailed much closer. She was in prime condition – paintwork bright, brasswork gleaming. No one came out on deck to observe his approach and still there was no sign of any swimmers. Could she have broken free from her moorings and drifted out to sea? If so, there was the chance of salvage money . . .

He brought his boat alongside, called out; there was no response. He secured his painter on a handy cleat, athletically hauled himself aboard despite his many years. Quickly, he made certain there was no one aboard. As he visually searched the surrounding sea, he wondered how much salvage would be worth when the boat must have cost almost as many pesetas as there were stars in the sky?

CHAPTER 6

Be not hasty or life will pass you by too quickly. It was not until Alvarez was thinking of leaving the office in the evening that the telephone rang and, reluctantly, he answered the call.

'It's Jorge Vaquer here. I've not seen you around for a long while.'

'I've been very busy.'

'But doing what, eh?' Vaquer laughed coarsely. 'So how's the family?'

They chatted for five minutes, then Alvarez said: 'Is there a problem?'

'I'm not certain. Do you know Santiago Fiol?'

'Hook-arse Santiago?' he asked, using the nickname by which Fiol had been known from the day when, a fifteen-year-old, he had cast a line which had left a fishhook deeply imbedded in the buttock of the boat owner.

'That's him. A real difficult bastard. All mooring fees were raised last year, but when I told him that he'd have to pay more, just like everyone else, he all but picked up a marlinspike to brain me.'

'What's he up to these days – running contraband cigarettes?'

'You think I'd tell you if he were?'

'I certainly hope not.'

'He was out beyond the heads in his boat this morning and saw a large motor cruiser. She wasn't under way and he wondered if there was trouble and closed, then boarded. She was unmanned.'

'What does that add up to?'

'Looks like she wasn't tied up properly – there's many a

29

boat owner who can't tell a sheepshank from a granny – and broke free and drifted out to sea even though there's been no wind and precious little current, or whoever was aboard went over the side for one reason or another and couldn't get back.'

'What's more likely?'

'There's no knowing at the moment.'

'Accidents aren't my problem.'

'Sure. But I reckoned you needed to know the facts.'

To cover his own responsibilities. Sometimes it seemed that in the modern world it was only self-interest which motivated people. And this selfish attitude meant that he might be landed with finding out what had happened. 'Who owns the boat?'

'Can't say. The papers should be aboard, of course, but they aren't; a lot of people keep 'em ashore in case their boat's pinched because no papers make her more difficult to sell illegally.'

'Have you seen it before?'

'She comes in occasionally to fuel or tie up for a short while.'

'Then the owner may live fairly locally?'

'I reckon.'

'Can you tell me anything about him?'

'Just that he's a typical foreigner who thinks because he's bloody rich, people ought to bow down to him.'

'Describe him.'

'Middle aged, but not beginning to rust since more often than not he has a young woman in tow who'd have you panting so hard your cojones would steam.'

'I don't pant.'

'You poor old sod!'

'You can't say for certain he's accidentally fallen overboard?'

'Haven't you been listening to a word I've been saying?'

'Just confirming. In the circumstances, there's nothing more I can do.'

'I'd have said you haven't done anything.'

'If you learn any more, you can let me know.'

'And waste my time?'

'Like me trying to make certain all the fees you collect reach the books?'

'Who's been spreading those lies?'

'A little bird.'

'I'll wring its bloody neck.'

Satisfied that verbal honours were even, Alvarez said goodbye and rang off.

Marti drove round the back of the outbuilding because the señor demanded that none of the staff's cars were left in sight of the main entrance, despite the fact that there was little parking space beyond the outbuilding, but a considerable amount in the front of the house. He picked up the plastic shopping bag from the passenger seat, climbed out of the car and walked round to the kitchen.

Rosa was preparing vegetables. As he put the bag on the table, she said: 'Did you get everything?'

'Yes.' It didn't worry him that she failed to thank him for his trouble. To help someone was a natural thing to do and therefore there was no call to be thanked.

'And the change?'

'Inside the bag.'

There was never any reluctance to ask directly about money for fear that to do so might suggest there was a doubt about another's financial honesty; since it was only relatively recently that Mallorquins had waved poverty goodbye, they kept a close watch on every peseta.

'Would you like some hot chocolate?' Rosa asked. 'And a croissant?'

'Best not. If I don't appear in the garden, the señor will start shouting his head off.'

'He won't, because he's still not back.' She left the stove and crossed to a working surface, opened a bread bin and brought out several croissants on a metal rack. She put one on a plate, placed this on the table. 'I made 'em yesterday evening, but they're still so fresh, you wouldn't know.' Because of the

31

distance to the nearest shop, she had frequent opportunity to exhibit her cookery skills. 'D'you want some butter?'

'Might as well.'

She brought butter on a dish from the large, double-door refrigerator. 'I'm worried, Gaspar.'

'What about?'

'Him being away all this time and no word. I know he don't bother to tell us much, but if he's not going to be here for a night, he usually says, so as I can make certain all the alarms are set.'

'Too busy chasing after the skirt to bother.'

She was unsurprised by his harsh tone of voice; since the death of Carolina, his daughter, he'd been able to see only the darkest side of life. Her own experience had taught her that to do this was to enclose oneself and the only antidote to mental pain was to look outwards, but she was certain that nothing she could say would change his attitude. 'He was supposed to meet Señorita Lockwood, but never turned up – she's rung more than once asking where he is. And where's his boat?'

'Wherever he is, like as not.'

'You don't think he could have had an accident? From what I've seen, Señorita Lockwood's leading him a bit of a dance and that's made him even more eager, so he'll be real keen not to upset her and since something must have stopped him seeing her Thursday night, surely he'd have phoned her if he could?'

He shrugged his shoulders.

She returned to the stove, picked up the jug in which she'd made the chocolate, carried this to the table and poured a mugful for herself. She sat on a second chair, stared into space. 'I'm wondering.'

'Forget the bastard.'

'Not about him. Whether I should have a croissant? The last time I weighed myself, I thought the machine had gone wrong.'

32

CHAPTER 7

Alvarez left the post and walked up to the old square, most of which was barricaded off because of the work that was going on. At the same time as the square was being reduced to rubble, houses were being knocked down so that the Calvario steps could be extended. Why? There had always been three hundred and sixty-five steps. A figure with significance. Now, many more were being added, increasing the total to a number without any significance. Why were there always people in the world who had to change something, either for a bad reason or for no reason at all?

The barman in the Club Llueso said: 'You look like your ticket in the primitive lottery was just one short.'

'I'm thinking what a crazy world we live in.'

'If it's taken you this long to find that out, small wonder you're in the Cuerpo.'

'Give me a café cortado and a large coñac.'

'Do I ever serve you anything but a large one?'

Alvarez carried glass and cup and saucer across to one of the window seats. He drank some coffee, then some brandy, poured the remaining brandy into the cup. He watched two slim, attractive, scantily clad young women until they passed out of sight. If only he were younger . . . Wishes were as useful as broken ploughshares. He finished the coffee and brandy and his mood lightened slightly; after a second brandy, he thought that perhaps it was the oddities which helped to make life worth living. And where was the point in being miserable on a Saturday? At weekends, he could enjoy a brandy or two extra before the meal, another glass or two of wine with the meal, and perhaps an hierbas after it to make certain he slept well throughout an extended siesta.

He had not been back in the office more than fifteen minutes when the phone rang. Attuned as he was to life's vagaries, instinct warned him his plans for the weekend were about to be disrupted. 'Yes?'

'I was told to ring you,' a woman said by way of introduction.

'Who told you?'

'The sargento.'

A slacker, always ready to bow down another's shoulders with the work he should be doing. 'Your name?'

'Rosa Camps. And you're Dolores's cousin. When I was in the village last week, I spoke to her and she told me all about the family . . .'

He would have liked to tell her to ring the sargento a second time and say that Inspector Alvarez was far too busy to concern himself with her problem. But if he were that unhelpful she might, since women caused trouble even when not trying, mention to Dolores that he must be a very busy man because he was so short on the telephone . . .

'. . . I'm glad Juan and Isabel are doing so well at school. You must be proud to have so clever a family.'

'Indeed . . . Now, how can I help?'

'I'm not certain.'

Typical! he thought.

'I could be wrong, of course. After all, you can't be certain how foreigners are going to act, can you?'

He gloomily stared up at the ceiling. Mention foreigners and in walked trouble.

'Perhaps he just didn't want to tell her that he wouldn't be turning up to see her.'

'Suppose you tell me exactly what's happened from the beginning.'

She did so.

He was about to explain why he would pass the problem on to someone else when he suddenly remembered the drifting motor cruiser. 'Do you know the name of the señor's yacht?'

'I should do.' There was a long pause. 'Something like *Valijero*, except I don't think it was quite that.'

34

'Mail carrier' did seem an unlikely name for a boat. 'You can't be more exact?'

'Not really.'

'Never mind. Thanks for telling me about this. I'll look into it right away.'

After ringing off, he congratulated himself on having given Rosa the impression of a man eager to help a friend of Dolores's; he checked the number of the harbourmaster's office in the port, dialled it. When the connection was made, he asked: 'What's the name of the boat that was found drifting out at sea?'

'*Valhalla.*'

The name was sufficiently similar to the one Rosa had suggested that he was reasonably certain he had identified the owner. 'Where is it at the moment?'

'She's tied up here.'

'I'll be down to have a look at it because I've just had a report of a man who may have gone missing. His housekeeper says he left his place on Parelona Peninsula on Thursday evening in his motor cruiser, and although she couldn't remember its name, she thought it was something like *Valijero.*'

'There's not much room for doubt, then. Fell overboard because he was too tight to remember that even with all his money, he couldn't walk on water.'

'Why d'you say he was tight?'

'There's an almost empty bottle of coñac and a glass with the remains of a drink in it by the bar in the saloon. Anyway, what weekend sailor's sober after he's been at sea for half an hour?'

'Sounds like you have to be right,' Alvarez said with relief. An incident this straightforward involving a foreigner wasn't going to disturb the pace of life very much.

He never ceased to be amazed by the boats in the port; not by the variations in shapes, sizes, and designs, not because there were people so stupid as to choose to put their lives at risk in conditions less salubrious than those found in jail, but by the hundreds of millions they had cost. And this was only one port on the island, the island only one yachting centre in the world. To realize that was to understand why an inspector in the Cuerpo was a financial nobody.

The harbourmaster's office was on what had originally been the eastern arm of the harbour when there had been no cat's-cradle of berths as there now was; it lay just beyond a restaurant whose menu made the mouth water, whose prices made the mind reel.

Vaquer, a large man with a jovial manner, but eyes which seldom laughed, shook hands. 'It's like a furnace today,' he said, as he mopped his face and neck with a handkerchief. 'I asked for air-conditioning, but they said it's too expensive to instal and run. Let 'em work in here for a morning and there'd be a unit installed before the end of the afternoon.'

'The bosses always keep cool.' If he were to finish work in time to enjoy the weekend to the full, there was no time for idle conversation. 'Where's the boat?'

'Tied up at the outer jetty.'

'Have you learned anything more about it?'

'Nothing.'

'Then let's go and have a look at it.'

'You don't need me . . .'

'Can't manage without you.'

Vaquer swore, then unwillingly followed Alvarez out of the office, which, thanks to the two fans running at full speed was cooler than he had suggested, and into the stifling heat outside.

They drove to the outside arm and along this, past several boats including a Chinese junk, to the end berth. Alvarez stared at the motor cruiser, in pristine condition, which had raked bows, a long foredeck, a bridge set slightly above the rest of the superstructure, glassed-in accommodation almost to the stern, and several portholes along the hull. 'She must have cost something!'

'Start at three, four hundred million.'

He whistled.

'And that's just the beginning. There's the mooring fees

and all the running expenses – bottom-scrubbing and anti-fouling, painting, repairs, updating electronic equipment – and the engines at speed will gulp down diesel quicker 'n you can empty a glass . . . Put your wages and mine together and they wouldn't keep her steaming long enough to reach the peninsula . . . So what do you want to do now?'

'Have a look around.'

'What's stopping you?'

The answer was something so pathetic that it would have needed burning spills under his fingernails to make him admit it. But for an altophobe even the suspicion of height or depth turned him into an arrant coward. The gap between the quayside and the hull was no more than a metre because the fenders were not large, the gangplank was narrow but secure, and nothing should have been easier than to cross; but there were no hand ropes and the drop might look small to another, but to him it was beginning to reach down to eternity . . .

'You may have all the time in the world to stand around, but I don't.' Vaquer crossed the gangplank with careless strides.

Only Alvarez knew the courage it took to walk the plank. When he stood on the deck, he was sweating so profusely it was as if the temperature had suddenly soared into the forties and he had difficulty in controlling the trembling of his arms.

'Where d'you want to go?'

'Everywhere.'

They viewed the engine room with twin diesels, then the crew's quarters in the bows – one small cabin for the captain and another for two hands, one head . . .

'One has to assume there were no crew aboard,' Alvarez said, as they made their way aft.

'This class of boat is designed for either owner sailing or, if he wants to go deep water, with a crew.'

'Would it be difficult to handle on one's own?'

'Not if one has a gram of seamanship.'

'Was there ever a crew in the past?'

'I've never seen any hands aboard. That's all I can say.'

They climbed a short companionway to reach the three large cabins and fully equipped bathrooms. The double bunk in the owner's cabin was made up, those in the other two cabins were stripped; there was nothing personal in any of them, or in the bathrooms.

In the large saloon-cum-smoke room there was a free-standing bar, along the outside edge of which ran a line of storm-holders, and in two of these were a glass, a quarter filled, and an uncapped bottle of Gran Reserva, all but empty.

'He'd expensive tastes,' Alvarez said, studying the bottle.

'D'you expect a man who owns a cruiser like this to drink gut-rot?'

'The meanest man I ever met was one of the richest.'

'But I'll bet he always saw himself all right.' Vaquer slumped down on one of the fixed stools in front of the bar.

'Why would he stop the engines?' Alvarez asked.

'Did you notice the stern davits?'

'The what?'

'Don't they teach you anything in the Cuerpo? On a craft like this, they're used to lower and hoist a tender. Well, the falls are slack and there's no tender on the chocks. So I'm saying that one engine caused trouble and instead of returning on the other, he decided to lower the dinghy or inflatable and use that to try to find out what was wrong with the starboard propeller.'

'Why should anything have been wrong?'

'When Diego and Marcelo went out to bring her in, Marcelo started the engines and tried to get under way, but it was obvious there was trouble with the starboard shaft or propeller. He told Diego to strip off and dive into the water to see if he could trace the problem. There was a length of line wrapped around the propeller.'

'So knowing that, what do you think happened with Vickers?'

'When he realized there was trouble, he decided to lower

the dinghy and try to locate what that was. Only being a landlubber, he didn't bother to make certain the painter was securely fast or that the cruiser had lost all way before the dinghy touched the water. So he saw it drifting free. Being pissed, instead of letting it vanish if he couldn't get the cruiser sailing – the only person aboard, there was no back-up – he went over the side to swim across. Only by then the dinghy was too far away for him to reach it and when he decided to return he found he hadn't the strength. Or maybe he managed to reach the cruiser, but just couldn't pull himself up and aboard.'

'What a way to go!'

'We've all got to go some way.'

'But not being able to climb up. Think of the growing panic.'

'You've too much imagination.'

It was obvious that Vaquer did not share his appreciation of the situation. To have safety so close and yet too far away, was to heighten the agony . . .

'If you've finished, you can take me back.'

Ironically, the trip back across the gangplank was not an ordeal because his mind was still fixed on an even greater horror.

They were driving past a large power boat flying the Panamanian flag when Vaquer said: 'Let me know if you ever find out for certain what happened.'

'Sure. I expect the body will turn up sooner or later.'

'I meant about the line around the propeller.'

'What's special about that?'

'Marcelo said it was wound around left-handed, but the propeller's right-handed.'

'What's that mean?'

'I've just told you, I'd like to know.'

'Make a guess.'

'He could have been going full astern when the line was caught up. But why would he have been doing that when out at sea?'

Alvarez braked to a halt by the office. 'Maybe he saw a pink elephant straight in front of it.'

'There's no one ever going to mistake you for even half a seaman,' Vaquer said as he climbed out of the car. He slammed the door shut, spoke through the opened window. 'Dead ahead, not straight in front of. And a boat's always she. D'you know why?'

'No idea.'

'The more screws she has, the faster she moves.'

The road twisted and turned, rose and fell, and at times there were vertiginous falls beyond its edges. Alvarez kept his gaze firmly ahead and tried not to imagine one of the tyres suffering a blow-out to send the car hurtling over a hundred-metre drop. However, when near the Parelona Hotel – once proudly exclusive, now having to cater to a broader clientele because wealth had reached earthy hands – the road levelled out and he was able to relax. For several kilometres there was not a single building, only solitude; then, just before the land once more rose, a sign 'Ca'n Mortice' directed him to the right.

He turned on to a dirt track that meandered between tall bushes, weeds and the occasional tree, then rose slightly before the house came in sight. He braked the car to a halt as he stared at the beauty of the small cove. He'd thought he'd enjoyed all the treasures of the island, but here was evidence that there were still jewels for him to discover. The owner of Ca'n Mortice lived with the gods – provided, that was, he hadn't found a watery grave.

He drove on and parked in front of the house, crossed to the square porch. The front door, shaped with a curving top, was panelled to a traditional Spanish design about which there was a hint of the ecclesiastical. He rang the bell and when Rosa opened the door, introduced himself.

'Have you found where he is?' she asked.

'I'm afraid not yet. But I have learned something which may be important which is why I'm here.'

'What?'

'Shall I come in?'

She was flustered because she thought it might have seemed to him that she had been showing bad manners

by not inviting him in. 'I'm sorry. Things are so difficult . . .'
She opened the door fully and stood to one side.

He entered a hall that at first glance seemed large enough
to encompass the whole ground floor of his home. Since a
hall was no more than a place of passage, to build one this
size showed extraordinary extravagance. Foreigners seemed
unable to grasp one of the most important facts of life, every
peseta needed to be made to do a peseta's work . . .

'You'd best come in here.'

The sitting room was much larger than the hall and delight-
fully cool, and as he enjoyed this escape from the oppressive
heat, he decided air-conditioning could never be called an
extravagance. The far end of the room was almost all glass and
much of the cove was visible – the sharp forms and different
shades of brown and grey of rock faces, the greens and faded
greens of undergrowth and of the pine trees which seemed
to grow out of the rock itself, the deep blue of the water
and the lighter blue of the sky which met at the short arc of
visible horizon, provided a different perspective, but equally
attractive picture, from that which he'd seen on his arrival.

She sat, nervously fiddled her fingers together. He settled
on one of the armchairs, thick with luxury. 'Do you remember that when you phoned, I asked you the name of the
señor's boat?'

She nodded.

'You weren't quite certain what it was, but suggested
something like *Valijero*. Could it have been *Valhalla*?'

'That's it,' she answered without hesitation.

'A large motor cruiser called *Valhalla* was found drifting at
sea yesterday.'

'And the señor?'

'There was no one aboard.'

'Is he dead?'

'Since there's been no sight of him since Thursday, I'm
afraid it looks as if he probably is.'

She crossed herself, but did so almost perfunctorily. He
was unsurprised. Not only was Vickers a foreigner, the older
Mallorquins, perhaps still close to their peasant roots, had not

been overcome by a hedonistic view of life and rejection of death, but accepted that the one had to end in the other so that tragedy was inevitable. 'It seems possible there was trouble with one of the propellers so he stopped the boat and lowered the dinghy, intending to find out what was wrong, only he hadn't secured it firmly and it drifted off and he decided to swim across to it. The distance became too great for him.'

'Surely he'd have had more sense than to do a thing like that?'

'He could have been drinking heavily – there was an almost empty bottle of brandy by the bar in the saloon. If that was full or nearly full when he started, he may have been incapable of rational judgement. Would you say he is a heavy drinker?'

'Not really. I mean, I can't say I've ever seen him completely tight.'

'Tell me about him. Describe the kind of man he is. Does he treat you pleasantly, is he generous, does he have many friends?'

Initially hesitant, she soon spoke freely. The señor – God rest his soul if he'd drowned – had not been a bad employer. Which was not, of course, to say that he had been a good one. He had paid good wages, but only because it was not everyone who would work in a house that was many, many kilometres from anywhere. He'd always increased their wages by more than the official rise in the cost of living, but so he should have because everyone knew that the government's figures were fiction . . . At the beginning of the week she'd driven to Llueso to buy a new frock, to find that everything cost almost twice as much as previously . . .

He listened stoically to the shopping saga and reflected on the fact that they were both referring to Vickers sometimes in the present, sometimes in the past; one minute alive, the next dead. Eventually, there was a pause. 'Is the señor married?'

'Yes, but they're separated and don't have anything to do with each other.'

'He lives on his own, then?'

'Only when he has to.'

'How d'you mean?'

'He has women friends. Always much younger than him and tarty-looking,' she added with a touch of verbal venom.

'Has he anyone at the moment?'

'The last one to live here left a while back and now he's after Señorita Lockwood – only she's not making it easy for him. But he'll get what he wants in the end. They see the house, the cars, the boat, the way he chucks the ten-thousand-peseta notes around. There's nothing like money, is there?'

'Never having had any, I wouldn't know.'

'Well, it's too late for you to find out.'

An unnecessary and inaccurate remark, he thought.

'I told Luisa, if the likes of her is invited to a meal at the Parelona Hotel, it's not because the food's good, it's to persuade her to forget to say no.'

'Who's Luisa?'

'She works here along with me, only she still lives at home and has to drive in from Llueso so doesn't come Saturdays unless there's a reason.'

'Does anyone else work here apart from her and the gardener you mentioned over the phone?'

'Not unless he gives a really big party. Then I've a cousin who comes along to give a hand.'

'Did anyone visit the señor on Thursday?'

'There was Señor Lovell, but that's all I saw. When I'm up in my room in the afternoon – I like a bit of a rest after working hard all morning – I don't know what goes on in the rest of the house. And there's many a time when that's a good thing!'

'Señor Lovell is a friend?'

'I suppose so.'

'You sound doubtful.'

'Well, I've only ever seen him here once before and that was some time ago.'

'How long?'

'Hard to say. Maybe three months. Could be less, could be more.'

44

'From what you've said, I take it that when he came on Thursday, it was in the morning?'

'That's right.'

'What can you tell me about the visit?'

'I don't rightly know how you mean.'

He explained. She told him Lovell had arrived and she'd shown him into the library, where Señor Vickers had been, and then she'd returned to the kitchen to make coffee. She'd taken that to them, Luisa being busy with cleaning.

'Were they behaving like old friends – you know, chatting away and cheerful?'

'Hardly.'

He waited.

'Even before I went in, I could hear the señor and that's unusual with the door being so thick. And even when I went in, he didn't stop right away.'

'Stop what?'

'Shouting. He's a temper and a half when he gets going.'

'They were having a row?'

'He was, that's for sure.'

'What about Señor Lovell?'

'He wasn't saying anything, but he looked right unhappy.'

'Have you any idea what the trouble was?'

She shook her head. 'When the señor starts shouting and talking twice as fast, I understand him hardly at all. I wasn't ever taught English and, working for foreigners, have just had to pick up what I can, which ain't much.'

'Did you see them again before Señor Lovell left?'

'No. When the señor rang the bell and told me to clear the coffee things from the library, Señor Lovell had already left . . . And you know what? The señor was smiling! Usually when he's been in a temper, it takes him an age to get over it. I once forgot to tell the store in Llueso he wanted some of his special champagne and when he went there they hadn't got any of it. He came back shouting and it wasn't until the next day he calmed down. Yet here he was, on Thursday, smiling. There's no understanding.'

'You know what they say. When God created humans, He

45

started the first lottery . . . When was the last time either you or Luisa saw the señor?'

'I suppose it was just before seven. He phoned through for some ice and I told Luisa to take it to him. Did she complain! Wanted to leave early as she and her novio were going out. I told her, she's paid to work to seven. What's more, the two of them would do better to save the money for marriage – that is if he really is thinking of marriage.'

'The señor wanted ice because he was going to have a drink?'

'Why else?'

He did not bother to explain that if Vickers had started drinking even before he set sail, it seemed very likely he had been too befuddled to deal sensibly with a problem at sea. 'And is that, as far as you know, the last she saw of him?'

'When she came back to the kitchen, she said she was off and went.'

'Did you see him after that?'

'No.'

'Has Gaspar mentioned seeing or talking to the señor that evening?'

'If he was paid for talking, he'd be as poor as a starving rat. And when he does say something, like as not it'll make you feel half as miserable as him. His wife and him belong to some sect that holds almost everything is a sin. Not that they'd have much to smile about even if they was encouraged to, not since their daughter died . . . When I heard about that, I told him how sad I was and all he could say was, life wasn't meant to be happy. And there's some truth in that if you're a woman.'

She was beginning to sound like Dolores and he hastened to move the conversation on. 'I need to talk to Señora Vickers and maybe Señorita Lockwood, so would you know their addresses and telephone numbers?'

'I don't know their addresses but the señora's number will be in the book; and come to think of it, the señorita gave me her number so that the señor could ring. I wrote it down and Luisa put it somewhere.'

46

'Would you look that out for me?'

She left the room, to return a few minutes later with a piece of paper which she handed to him. She said: 'There's worse employers around, even if he is like a dog after a bitch. I hope he's not dead.'

Something of a mixed epitaph?

CHAPTER 9

As Alvarez approached the roundabout on the eastern edge of Llueso, he accepted he must phone Señora Vickers, however disturbing that proved to be (separation did not always bring to an end all emotion). But, he went on to ponder, might it not be best to wait to do so in case fresh evidence came to hand so that he could give the señora definite news? And if he returned to the office, he'd have to find somewhere to park, which was becoming more difficult by the day, the call might prove to be a long one, and he could well not arrive home before lunch was over . . . At the roundabout, he took the Laraix road and was home within five minutes.

Jaime was seated at the table in the dining room and Juan and Isabel were watching the television. Alvarez settled opposite Jaime, opened the sideboard and brought out a glass, poured himself a brandy to which he added three cubes of ice.

With a jerk of the head in the direction of the bead curtain, Jaime said, in a low voice: 'She was fussing just now. Said if you stayed in the bar much longer, you'd miss lunch.'

'I haven't been near a bar. I've been working flat out all morning.'

'On a Saturday?'

'Work comes before pleasure.'

'Tell her that and she'll laugh in your face.'

'It's fact. A motor cruiser was found drifting at sea with no one on it and no way of identifying the owner, but earlier I learned about an Englishman who could have gone missing. I've been trying to find out if the boat's his and he's fallen over the side and drowned.'

'Who is he?'

'His place is on the way to the Parelona lighthouse and there isn't another for kilometres. It overlooks a cove more beautiful than you can imagine.'

'So he's rich?'

'Rich enough to live in a place like that, own a large boat, and call on beautiful young women any time he feels the urge.'

'It's all wrong!'

Surprised by the force with which the other had spoken, Alvarez said curiously: 'Are you becoming all moral?'

'Why should he have everything and the likes of us, nothing?'

The bead curtain parted and Dolores stepped into the room. She studied Alvarez. 'You are finally here! Did the bar close because you had drunk it dry?'

'I haven't been near a bar all morning . . .'

'Do you also wish me to believe in fairies?'

'I've had a really heavy morning . . .'

'And you think I have not? You believe a meal arrives at the table of its own accord; that I have spent the hours sitting, reading the paper? Ayee! If I were not a woman who never complains, I would have something to say!'

Juan spoke up. 'I can't hear the telly with all the talking.'

She swung round. 'What's that?'

Belatedly, he realized his mistake. 'It's just that it's my favourite programme,' he answered meekly.

'And that gives you the right to be rude to your mother?'

Juan looked to his sister for moral support; she smiled with open satisfaction.

'You perhaps believe yourself to be almost a man so you can be rude to any woman whenever you wish?'

'I wasn't . . .'

'Up to your room!'

'But why?'

'To reflect on your wickedness.'

'That's unfair . . .'

'Were you a woman, you would know that life is never fair. I spend all morning slaving in the kitchen, doing the work of three, your father and your uncle – when he remembers where he lives – sit at the table, doing the work of none, drinking, so that it is I who am left to teach you manners. Up to your room and do not come down until I call you.'

After aiming a kick at his sister's legs which missed, Juan crossed to the stairs and stamped his way up them.

Head held high, Dolores returned into the kitchen where she banged dishes around to express her feelings.

Alvarez said, in a low voice: 'So what's suddenly got her in this mood?'

'How would I know?' Jaime answered.

'I suppose it's something you've said or done.'

'No, it bloody isn't. I'll tell you exactly what it is – you. Trying to make out you were working when you've been in a bar.'

Why, Alvarez wondered, was a lie so often easier to believe than the truth?

He awoke, certain he had enjoyed happy dreams, though unable to remember a single detail. He opened his eyes and stared up at the ceiling, on which were patterned bars of light reflected up by sunshine through the closed shutters, and luxuriated in the fact that there was no need to move since it was a Saturday . . .

'Enrique,' Dolores called up from downstairs, 'it's late. Are you ever coming down?'

Women seemed unable to relax.

'I'm going out in a few minutes and after that you'll have to make your own coffee.'

He got off the bed, put on shirt, pants, trousers and sandals, and hurried downstairs. He sat at the table in the centre of the kitchen.

'There's some coca in that cupboard.' She pointed, then spooned coffee into the machine. 'When I leave here, I'm going to see Eva.'

'Eva Hopeful?'

'What's that?'

'Just a little joke.'

51

'I've told you before, your jokes are ridiculous.'

'Sorry,' he mumbled.

'Her husband's been dead two years, but she still wears black.' She screwed the lid of the machine on to its base. 'I've told her, it's time for grey and in another year, some colour. Things are very different now from how they were when a widow wore black until she died. Wouldn't you agree?'

'Indeed.'

'Do you know what she replied? "Who do I have to wear colour for?" Isn't that sad?'

'Very.' He was becoming uneasily certain that this conversation was not as aimless as her manner suggested.

'She never could have any children and she has so few living relatives that a distant cousin is the nearest; she does not like him. So she is alone, living in a big house with a great deal of land and no one to share everything with her.'

He decided that he must make it clear he would not court Eva. 'That's hardly surprising.'

'What do you mean?'

'Did you never hear Miguel say what life with her was like?'

'I do not listen to malicious gossip.'

'She has a disposition like a bull that's been pricked.'

'Married to him, even a saint would have cause to swear.'

'And she'll never win a beauty contest.'

Dolores's annoyance finally surfaced. 'Typical! Like any man, you cannot look beyond a pretty face! If she were a twenty-year-old blonde with dewy eyes and the kind of body you dream about when you think there is no one around to read your smirking expression, you would rush to comfort her loneliness.'

'If she were all that, she would not be lonely.'

'Men!' she said with sharp distaste.

'What I'm trying to say is –'

'I have much more important things to do than listen to what you have to say. And now I have no time to put the coffee on the stove.' She crossed to a stool and picked up her handbag from it, left the kitchen through the rear doorway

52

that gave access to a small courtyard and the passage that ran back to the road.

He put the coffee machine on the stove, lit the gas. To say what he had was bound to have annoyed her, but there had been no other way of convincing her that he was not interested in Eva. The Good Lord knew how much he longed to own land, to run his fingers through the soil, to sew and to reap, to pluck fruit from trees, but not only had Miguel said she'd a temper that could curdle milk, she'd also made it clear to him some years before that she wasn't going to put up with any more of that nonsense in bed.

As Alvarez entered the post, the duty cabo said: 'Coming to work on a Saturday afternoon! Have pigs started to fly?'

'They still sit at desks and do nothing.'

In his office, Alvarez spent several minutes staring at the telephone as he tried to find a reason for postponing the call; finally, he sighed, checked the piece of paper Rosa had given him, dialled the first number written on it.

'I'd like to speak to Señora Vickers. Inspector Alvarez, Cuerpo General de Policia,' he said, when the connection was made.

There was a pause. 'Is there a problem?' a man asked.

'I'll discuss that with the señora.'

'Yes, of course. I'll get her.'

Those few words, because of the way in which they'd been spoken, had built up in Alvarez's mind a man who met any authority, however minor, with downcast eyes. He waited, receiver to his left ear, wishing he were doing anything but this. A man's mental strength was tested to the limit when he had to tell a wife – even a separated one – that she might soon have to accept that she was a widow . . .

'What is it?' asked a woman in slow, carefully constructed Spanish that was not easy to understand because of a heavy accent.

'Señora, have you heard from your husband in the last two days?' he asked in English.

'No. Nor would I expect to. Why do you ask?'

53

'I am sorry to have to tell you that it seems he is missing.'

'Missing in what way?'

'Since Thursday evening, when it has to be assumed he sailed from his home in his motor cruiser, he has not been seen.'

'Try Monaco. That's his favourite trysting spot because he's naive enough to believe it's as glamorous as people say it is.'

Her misconception was not making his task any easier, but he was already certain that what he had to tell her would not affect her nearly as much as he had feared. 'I very much regret that his boat was found drifting at sea and there was no one on it.'

After a while, she said: 'Are you telling me that he fell overboard and drowned?'

'That seems sadly probable. But I must add that there is no certainty this was the case, which is why I am here to ask if you can help me.'

'I'm almost the last person to be able to do that. I suggest you speak to whichever woman is his present flavour of the month.'

'Recently, he has been living on his own.'

'Not by choice, that's for certain.'

'You cannot suggest where he might be now, assuming he did not suffer an accident and fall overboard?'

'No.'

The task had proved far, far less stressful than he had feared – separation had marked a total break of emotion. 'Rest assured, señora, that when I learn something more, I shall be in touch.' He said goodbye and rang off. If she was now a widow, there had to be the possibility that she was a very wealthy widow . . .

He dialled Melanie Lockwood's number; an answerphone told him to leave a message when the beeps finished, so he replaced the receiver. He altered the angle of the fan to try to gain more benefit from its rushing wind, slumped back in the chair. He must make a report to Salas. Did he do that now, proving that when necessary he worked through weekends? But Salas was a man who concentrated on the minutiae of a case and demanded instant answers to every possible question and some that were impossible. What was the state of mind of Vickers before his disappearance? Had his visitor on the Thursday morning been questioned? Why not? . . . Clearly, the visitor must be questioned before Salas was briefed, but what had Rosa said his name was? . . . Foreigners observed weekends with appropriate zeal and so there could be little point in trying to engage the other's attention before Monday . . .

It was time to return home. Supper might well prove to be . . . He suddenly remembered what had happened before he'd left and he cursed himself for his stupidity in annoying Dolores – womanlike, suffering a sense of personal affront merely because her wishes had been politely denied, she might well have decided to serve a rag-and-bone meal as a small-minded gesture of angry retaliation. He'd better buy a large bunch of flowers on his way home and perhaps a box of chocolates as well. The last thing any of them wanted was several meals, none of which was any more appetizing than sopa de carboner.

CHAPTER 10

He phoned Ca'n Mortice on Monday morning and spoke to Rosa, who asked him if there was any more news. 'I'm afraid not.'

'Then he must surely be dead.' She spoke with the practical acceptance of someone who had suffered disappointment, disillusionment and tragedy.

'I think so, but there still has to be room for doubt . . . Rosa, what was the name of the man who came to the house on Thursday morning?'

'Señor Lovell.'

'And do you know where he lives or is staying?'

She named Ca Na Atalla and was able to tell him roughly where it was. He thanked her, rang off, checked the time. Probably, Lovell would be up by now, but one could never be certain where foreigners were concerned, so it must be advisable to wait before driving to the house. He'd had a cup of coffee and a brandy at Club Llueso an hour before, but that was no good reason for not having both again while he waited.

Rosa's description of the house's situation proved to be easily misunderstood and it needed an old man, looking after a small herd of sheep and lambs, to direct him up a narrow dirt track. Beyond a rock gateway and a turning circle, bordered by oleanders on one side and almond trees on the other, was a large, two-floor house with the usual jumble of roof lines. He parked the car and crossed to the four steps which brought him up to a small porch. He rang the bell at the side of the panelled door.

Beatriz, middle aged, heavy featured, opened the door.

When he asked if Señor Lovell was in, she nodded, told him to enter and to wait in the hall. When she returned, she was accompanied by a tall, well-built man, wearing smart, casual clothes. She went through the doorway to her left, he came to a halt and said in reasonable Spanish: 'Good morning. My name is Esme Dale. Beatriz said you're a detective. Is something wrong?'

'That is what I'm trying to find out, señor.'

'A somewhat enigmatic answer! . . . Come on through to the sitting room.' Once inside, he said: 'Perhaps you would like to be a little more explicit?'

'It is possible there has been a serious accident, but because that is not yet certain, I am making inquiries.'

'Like most enigmas, this one vanishes as soon as the facts are known . . . You want to speak to my cousin?'

'To Señor Lovell.'

'He's my cousin . . . Inspector, I don't quite know how to put this tactfully – that may well be impossible – but my cousin is, on his own admission, a man of some importance and therefore wholly unused to dealing with matters of small moment. Do you follow the gist of what I'm saying?'

'I am afraid not.'

'Then I will have to be frank, which is often a pleasure. When Beatriz said there was a detective who wished to speak to him, my cousin's response was that since there was no conceivable reason why a detective could need to do that, he was not going to waste his time. I hasten to add that he was not trying to be rude; those in high places unfortunately are so occupied by matters of great state that they really do find tremendous difficulty in appreciating that there can be matters of small state.'

'Of course, señor. So perhaps you will explain to Señor Lovell that it must be in his own interests to speak with me.'

'You are clearly a keen observer of human psychology and know that a politician will always respond enthusiastically to his own interests . . . Let me pass on your message.'

Dale crossed to the French windows and went out on to the covered patio, turned left to pass out of sight.

Alvarez's mind drifted. This area had been known as La Huerta de Llueso – the fruit or kitchen garden of Llueso. Now, surely a better name would be La Desierta de Llueso – the desert of Llueso. Foreigners with pockets filled with money had bought the fincas, the casetas, the fields, and converted or built until hardly any of the land was farmed as it had once been, with every square centimetre tilled, because only then could the tiller hope to make enough to be able to house and feed his family. Gone was the pride on growing; gone the satisfaction of seeing one's son draw his first straight furrow behind the ancient mule and Roman plough. Now, pride lay in bank accounts and new cars . . .

A man came into sight, opened the French windows and stepped inside. 'I trust this matter genuinely is important.'

The words had not been openly aggressive, the tone had. A man, Alvarez thought, who saw himself elevated well above the common herd. 'Señor Lovell, I'm sorry to bother you . . .'

'It will waste far less time for you to explain why you are.'

'I am inquiring into the possibility that Señor Vickers has unfortunately had a serious accident.'

Lovell turned and faced the French windows, jammed his hands into the pockets of his sharply creased linen trousers. After a moment, he said, without looking round: 'What kind of accident?'

'You haven't heard?'

'Would I ask if I had?'

'On Thursday evening, we can be almost certain that he sailed in his boat to meet a friend, but never arrived. On Friday, his boat was found adrift at sea without anyone on it. Since then, no one who might be expected to hear from him has done so. The facts have to suggest that he fell overboard.' Alvarez waited for a comment, but there was none. 'And drowned.'

'A natural consequence. Regrettable, of course, naturally,

but I fail to understand why you should come here and wish to speak to me on a matter that cannot possibly concern me.'

'Was he not a friend of yours?'

'No.'

'But you did visit his home?'

'I visit the homes of many people who I would never describe as friends.'

'You went there on Thursday morning, I believe?'

'And if I did?'

'What was the purpose of your visit?'

'That is my business.'

'It may well be important.'

'Important, or not, it will remain my business.'

'Señor, I need to try to appreciate the state of mind of Señor Vickers on Thursday since that may be very pertinent.'

'I cannot help you.'

'But I think you can because –'

'I am in no way responsible for the course of your thoughts.'

'I understand that you and he had a row that morning.'

'Your understanding is incorrect.'

'Rosa has told me that you and Señor Vickers were arguing.'

'Who is she?'

'The elder of the maids.'

'I am not in the habit of having my word challenged by a domestic.'

'Why would she make up such a story?'

'I have no idea.' He pulled his right hand out of his trouser pocket as he crossed to the French windows; he took hold of the handle.

'Señor, I have not finished.'

'I have.'

'If you would please –'

'Presumably, you are unaware that I am a member of the British government.'

'I did not know that, señor.' How much more satisfying

60

it would have been to say that he was making all due allowances for the fact. 'But nevertheless, I still have to ask you certain questions . . .'

'Which I do not have to answer.'

'On the contrary . . .'

'Your attitude is becoming somewhat unfortunate.'

'Señor, I am trying to be polite . . .'

'With signal lack of success.' Lovell went out on the patio, closed the door behind himself.

There were echoes of Salas in Lovell. Clearly, men in high places suffered the same delusions of self-importance whatever their nationality.

CHAPTER 11

Alvarez leaned back in his chair and tried to decide how he would spend the three hundred and fifty million pesetas he would surely win in the next draw of the primitive lottery? He'd buy a finca, of course; perhaps up the Laraix valley because there much of the land was good and there was plenty of water. But the valley was popular with the type of foreigner who bought a traditional house, attractive because it was so functionally simple, and paid many millions of pesetas to have it modernized and altered until it could boast his wealth. Then should he buy around Mestara? The village was in the central plain, the land was the richest on the island, and few foreigners lived in the area, but Mestarans were a sullen lot whose habits were at best dubious, at worst down-right reprehensible. A Mestaran wife would plough behind a mule; as every Llusian husband recognized, a woman that shameless would think nothing of planting a cuckold's horns on his head. A mountain property? There were many small valleys where the land could support farming and the people were almost untouched directly by the baleful influences of tourism, but the roads were unfenced despite sheer drops on one side or the other and to enjoy a quiet moment in a bar, one had to drive tortuous, dangerous kilometres. Life never willingly gave man an easy run. The desirable always had to be shadowed by the undesirable . . .

The phone rang.

'The superior chief,' said the secretary in her plum-filled voice, as if announcing royalty.

Salas never concerned himself with social pleasantries when dealing with subordinates. 'What the devil have you been up to this time?'

'How do you mean, señor?'

'How very typical! Even making all necessary allowances, I find it incredible that you have to ask that question.'

'Is this anything to do with Señor Lovell?'

'Are there so many to whom you have been insolent that you need a specific complainant to be identified?'

'I was not insolent to him . . .'

'Señor Lovell, acting with the tact and forbearance to be expected on the part of someone who is a not unimportant member of his government, as he modestly told me, made it clear that he did not wish his words to be taken as a formal complaint; indeed, he had the politeness to point out how ridiculous it would be to complain about the course of justice in a sovereign democratic country which honours the rule of law as enthusiastically as his own. But he thought it right, as a matter of tactful kindness, to point out that in the age of the common man there are many who are not alive to the subtleties and therefore he was bringing the matter to our attention in case we felt that steps should be taken to prevent any chance of future resentment on the part of someone less capable of understanding than he . . . What do you have to say?'

'Señor Lovell must indeed be a very great politician.'

There was a silence which Salas finally broke. 'At times I am totally perplexed by the fact that you were accepted into the Cuerpo, even though this occurred at a time when standards were lowered in order to encourage minorities . . . Could you not divine from his manner that Señor Lovell is a very important member of the British government?'

'I didn't have to guess that, señor. He told me.'

'Perhaps because he could understand the necessity for doing so. Yet despite this knowledge, you treated him with a complete lack of respect?'

'I showed him as much as I show anyone.'

'Good God, man, are you suggesting it's suitable to address a person in his position in the same way as a local peasant?'

'Provided I simplify everything.'

'What's that?'

'Just a little joke,' Alvarez murmured apologetically.

'What have I done to deserve this?' Salas shouted. 'An inspector who has been insolent to an important member of the British government and then jokes about it!'

'Señor, I took great pains to be polite . . .'

'Why were you questioning him?'

'To find out if he could help me make a judgement concerning the state of Señor Vickers's mind since that might indicate the likelihood of suicide.'

'Suicide of whom?'

'Señor Vickers.'

'He's dead?'

'I don't yet know for certain.'

'And are there many more whom you are considering as possible suicides even though you have no idea whether they are dead or alive?'

'It's because the boat was found drifting at sea and no one aboard –'

'What boat?'

'Señor Vickers's.'

'Alvarez, my job at all times is a very difficult one; after even a short report from you, it threatens to become an impossible one.'

'Perhaps if I started at the beginning?'

'You think yourself capable of so rational an experiment?'

Alvarez began a résumé of the facts, but was soon interrupted.

'The boat was found on Friday?'

'Yes, señor.'

'I do not recall your report concerning the matter.'

'There seemed to be no point at the time in making one.'

'Despite standing orders? Or is that, considering I am speaking to you, too naive a question? Even if you are aware there are such things, I suppose it's doubtful you have ever bothered to read them.'

'At the beginning, it was just a boat which had broken free. We couldn't even determine who owned it. And, until

Señora Rosa Camps told me Señorita Lockwood had phoned a couple of times –'

'Who is Señora Camps?'

'One of Señor Vickers's maids.'

'And Señorita Lockwood?'

'I suppose one could call her the señor's girlfriend, except Rosa reckons he probably hasn't yet scored . . .'

'Why have we wandered into a discussion about football?'

'Football?'

'That is what I said.'

'I'm afraid I don't understand.'

'Proust wrote that the most instructive conversation was one which neither participant really understood. I have always thought until now that only an author could write such nonsense, but I begin to understand what he was getting at. Can you explain how Vickers could possibly have scored if not playing football of one kind or another?'

'Well, it's . . . it's not . . . it's not exactly a reference to any game, señor. Unless, of course, one does see it as a game. Scoring is a way of saying, getting a woman into bed.'

'I should have remembered that you have an infinite capacity for unnecessary salacious details.'

'It might be important.'

'Perhaps to someone whose mind can, without exaggeration, be compared to a sewer.'

'But if, as Rosa suggests, she had been playing look-but-no-touch –'

'What in the devil are you talking about now?'

Alvarez sighed. 'The señor was – or is – obviously a very randy man –'

'Keep your language decent even if you cannot control your thoughts.'

'He's greatly attracted to beautiful young ladies and because he's very wealthy, he usually doesn't find any difficulty in making . . . in gaining their very close friendship . . .'

'I dislike the modern tendency towards cynicism.'

'As far as I can gather, Señorita Lockwood was not so eager . . . so easily impressed as many and was keeping him

. . . making certain the friendship didn't become too close, too quickly. This would have made him much more eager, wouldn't it?'

'I am happy to say that I have no idea.'

'Assume it would, then surely he wouldn't consider suicide on his way to a meeting when there was a chance he'd finally . . . when their friendship might flourish?'

'Earlier, you indicated that the reason for your questioning Señor Lovell was to determine the state of Vickers's mind in order to decide whether or not suicide was likely?'

'Yes, señor.'

'Yet now you claim it was very unlikely.'

'You have always said, señor, that if one is to conduct a good investigation, one has to consider every possibility, even contradictory ones.'

'The germane word is "good" and hardly applicable in this instance. You have managed to muddle all the facts, probably in your pursuit of salacious details, and have disgraced the Cuerpo by your insolence towards an important member of the British government.'

'I don't think that's fair –'

'I am not concerned with your opinion.' Salas cut the connection.

Alvarez replaced the receiver. It was stupid to resent Salas's unjust attitude – a common trait amongst seniors – but what did irk him was the fact that if he'd known Salas was not going to pursue the question of the state of Vickers's mind, he need not have visited Ca Na Atalla and would have avoided the meeting with Lovell which was causing so much trouble . . .

The phone rang again and he lifted the receiver.

'In what state are Vickers's finances?' Salas demanded.

He felt like a man who had been twice struck by lightning in direct contradiction to popular belief. 'In what way, señor?'

'Have you investigated bank balances, investments, debts?'

'No, señor.'

'It has not occurred to you that there may be a reason for Vickers to fake his own death? And if he were aware

67

that you would be in charge of the investigation into his disappearance, he will have been assured his chances of success must be high.' The connection was cut.

He would have considered the possibility, Alvarez assured himself. Once it was quite certain Vickers was missing and not busy scoring on an away pitch . . . When a man was, or had been, as wealthy as Vickers, one thing was certain – in order to avoid paying taxes, the other's financial affairs would be a cat's-cradle. So was he doomed to spend hour after hour poring over facts and figures while not understanding a quarter of them? A proposition to daunt the stoutest heart. A proposition to send a man to Club Llueso to find the courage he would need if he were to meet the future.

CHAPTER 12

'You're down at a reasonable time for once,' Dolores said.

Alvarez looked at the clock on the far wall of the kitchen.

'Much better for you,' she said, with the brisk certainty of someone who never allowed herself a long siesta.

'I need a lot of sleep.'

'Only because you drink too much.'

He felt too weary to argue further. 'Is there some coffee?'

'Not until I've made it.'

He sat.

'Why are you down now?' she asked, as she spooned ground coffee into the machine.

'Work.'

'You've never let that disturb you in the past.'

'There has to be a first time.'

'But sadly, never a last one.'

Her tone alerted him to what lay behind the sharp comments. 'I suppose you imagine I've cut my siesta short because I'm chasing after a sixteen-year-old?'

'My thoughts are my own.'

'Then it might be a good idea if you kept them to yourself,' he said, annoyance overtaking prudence.

She held her head a little higher.

'I am not interested in sixteen-year-olds.'

'As you are not interested in drinking? . . . Did you believe I didn't see you with that American child when you were trying to hide in the doorway of the paper shop?'

'My God! Let a woman see a worm and she shouts snake. She was not American, but Italian; she was nearer thirty than sixteen.'

'Italian children must age very quickly.' She put the coffee machine on the stove, lit the gas under it.

'Why do you go on and on at me like this?'

She crossed to one of the wall cupboards, opened the door, brought out a plate on which was a portion of coca, wrapped in cling; she removed the cling, put the plate down on the table in front of him with more force than was necessary. 'Honey or jam?'

'Just explain why you keep accusing me of chasing women young enough to be my daughters?'

'Do you want honey or jam?'

'And even if I were, which I most definitely am not, you seem to forget that I'm over twenty-one.'

'Every year a man gains makes him a little more foolish,' she snapped as she put two pots down on the table.

'I can't remember the last time I spoke socially to a young woman.'

'In the square when you were trying to hide from me.'

He gave up. There was no escape from taxes, death, and a woman's tongue.

'Are you capable of pouring out the coffee when it's ready?' she asked.

'I suppose I might just be able to if I concentrate really hard.'

She picked up her handbag, left.

He cut a slice of coca, spread jam thickly over it, ate. It was true that once or twice he had become friendly with foreign women who might have been a year or two younger than he. And perhaps each relationship had ended sadly, as Dolores had prophesied, but it was totally wrong to believe, as she claimed, that age difference had had anything to do with the break-up . . . Even if he had met Francisca before that day in the square, it was ludicrous to draw any assumption from the fact. And if he had hoped to shield her from Dolores's X-ray gaze, that had only been to avoid precisely what had just occurred, a ridiculous travesty of the truth . . . If only Francisca had not had to return to Rimini . . .

A hissing note from the stove brought his mind back to

the present. He had allowed the coffee to boil, which meant a little had dribbled out and down the side of the machine. He hurriedly stood, crossed to the stove, picked up the machine and promptly dropped it because he'd forgotten that the handle's insulation was poor. It fell on to its side and the contents gushed out. He swore. He'd lost the coffee, burned his hand, and would have to clean the stove because Dolores kept it gleaming. If she'd done her job and waited to pour out the coffee for him, none of this would have happened . . .

He parked in front of Ca'n Mortice, climbed out of the car and stared past the corner of the house at the segment of the cove that was visible. If one lived here, would, could, there come a time when one was no longer dazzled by the beauty of the scene? He hoped not.

Luisa opened the front door; he introduced himself, said there were a few questions he wanted to ask her.

'I can't help,' she said nervously.

'Not directly, of course, but perhaps indirectly.' When she made no move, he said: 'Shall I come in?' He entered, shut the door. There were those who said money couldn't buy happiness, but it certainly bought air-conditioning – seconds after stepping into the hall, he enjoyed the pleasure of feeling cool for the first time that day.

Rosa appeared. 'Have you heard something about the señor?'

He explained that nothing more was known and he had come to the house to speak to her and to Luisa in the hopes that one or the other of them might be able to offer a fresh lead.

'We was about to make ourselves some coffee – maybe you'd like some?'

'I would indeed.'

'D'you mind having it in the kitchen?'

'Where else?'

As they entered the kitchen, Rosa said: 'Which of us d'you want to talk to first?'

'Luisa.'

'Then I'll make the coffee. And how about a little coñac with it?'

'There's no need to ask twice.'

'Looking at you, I didn't think there would be!'

A shade too forthright in her observations, but her instincts were good. He sat on one of the rush-seated chairs, waiting until Luisa, after an initial hesitation, did the same, then said: 'Rosa's told me that on Thursday evening, she asked you to take some ice to the señor.'

Before Luisa could respond, Rosa said: 'And she didn't want to because she was in a hurry to be off to see her novio.'

'So you mentioned.'

'I told her, give it time and there won't be any rush!'

'It won't never be like that,' Luisa said, with some heat.

'It's always like that.'

He could be certain Dolores would have agreed. 'Can you say what the time was when you took the ice to the señor?'

'It was coming up to seven,' Rosa answered.

'I'm sorry, but I need to hear from Luisa what she thinks the time was.'

'Her generation don't spend much time thinking.'

'You've no right to talk like that,' Luisa snapped.

It was obvious that their relationship had become strained, perhaps because of their uncertain future. He said lightly: 'The problem is, I can't question both of you at the same time.'

'Only trying to help,' Rosa muttered.

He spoke to Luisa. 'Would you agree it was nearly seven when you took the ice through to the señor?'

'I suppose so.'

'Where was he?'

'In the sitting room.'

'What was he doing?'

'Waiting for the ice.'

A logical, if unhelpful answer! 'Had he been drinking before you went in?'

'How would I know?'

'You might have noticed his glass had something in it, or he might have been talking thickly.'

'He always did. I mean, English always sound thick.'

Patiently he continued the questioning. In truth, she didn't reckon the señor could have been drinking heavily; if she'd thought that, she'd have been very worried that he might make a pass at her . . .

Rosa's expression suggested she'd have to see stones melt before that was likely.

'Did you notice what he was drinking?'

'Can't say I did,' Luisa answered. 'Coñac, I suppose.'

'It can't have been,' Rosa said. Then, thinking Alvarez must be about to object to this further interruption, said hastily: 'It couldn't have been coñac.'

'Why not?' he asked casually, certain she could have no idea how important her answer might be.

'Because he reckoned that was what was upsetting him. I could have told him it was much more likely all the rich food he insisted on eating, but he'd never have listened.'

'And so he stopped drinking coñac?'

'That's what he said.'

'When did he tell you this?'

'Must have been about the beginning of last week, 'cause it was this week he said how much better he was feeling.'

Tradition held that every criminal made at least one mistake. Was the bottle of Gran Reserva left out in the saloon of the *Valhalla* the murderer's one? He turned to Luisa. 'When you took the ice to him, was he on his own?'

'No one came to the house in the afternoon or evening.'

'So he was on his own?'

'Of course he was.'

'Don't be saucy,' Rosa said as she poured coffee into three mugs.

'No offence meant, none taken.' He smiled. 'Tell me, Luisa, could you see if more than one glass was out and being used?'

She shrugged her shoulders. 'I didn't notice.' Her tone was sullen, as if she thought she was somehow being criticized.

'Whilst you were in the room, did he pour himself a drink?'

'No.'

'That's about everything, then. Thanks for your help.'

She looked puzzled, as if wondering how she could have helped.

He spoke to Rosa. 'You've told me about the row with Señor Lovell.'

'That's right.'

'You're sure it was a real row and not just a reasonably good-natured argument?'

She put milk and sugar on the table. 'I'd call it a row. Wouldn't you?' she asked Luisa. 'You told me you'd heard them when you passed the library.'

'Yeah.'

'I mean, most times you can't hear a thing from the library because the door's nice and thick, but there was this shouting that was quite loud.'

'You could hear both men?'

'I've told you before.'

'Tell me again.'

'I only heard the señor. When he gets annoyed, it's a real temper!'

'Have you any idea what the argument was about?'

'How could I when the door's so thick it muffles voices and then when I was in the room, the señor was going on at such a rate. It's like I said before. I'm not trying to lie.'

'Not for one moment do I think you are. But there's a bit of a problem here, so maybe you can help me solve it. Señor Lovell says there was no row between him and Señor Vickers; if anyone suggests there was, that person is mistaken.'

'He can say what he likes. I know what I hear and you know what you hear, don't you?' Rosa demanded as she turned to face Luisa.

'That I do! And you don't want to take any notice of Señor Lovell, not when he reckons people like us are little more than a piece of shit.'

'I don't want to hear that kind of language in my kitchen,' Rosa said sharply.

'It's you who told me that's how he'd spoken to you.'

'There was only you and me and not a man listening.'

'I have heard the word before,' he assured her. 'Well, I don't think I need bother you any more . . . By the way, a little earlier on, did you mention a small coñac to go with the coffee?'

CHAPTER 13

As Alvarez drove into the turning circle in front of Ca Na Atalla, a man who had been weeding one of the flower beds stood up; he recognized the other and after getting out of the car crossed to have a chat. It was a quarter of an hour later before he climbed the steps to the small patio and rang the front door bell.

Dale opened the door. 'Hullo, again. I'm sorry you've had to return. I did try to explain to my cousin that different lands, different customs, and even called into support the country where the classical two-finger salute is a friendly gesture, but I failed to convince him. As a committed European, he lacks a sense of the absurd. I do hope you haven't to make anything more than a brief, formal apology?'

'Apology, señor?'

'Isn't that why you're here?'

'I have to ask Señor Lovell one or two more questions.'

'Your senior officers are clearly men of sufficient common sense to have ignored my cousin's complaints!'

'Not quite. My superior chief has certainly suggested I was not as diplomatic as he would have wished.'

'He spoke in no more robust terms than those?'

Alvarez did not answer.

'You have decided to ignore the rebuke?'

'There is fresh evidence which makes it necessary to speak to Señor Lovell again.'

'Then come on through to the sitting room.'

He followed Dale into the large, cool room. Through the French windows, he could see Lovell, seated in the shade of a sun umbrella, working at a laptop.

Dale nodded in the direction of his cousin. 'I'm certain he

doesn't really understand that machine, but everyone in the government has been given one and told to work on it in order to be able to persuade the public that he or she is literate – computer literate, that is, since otherwise there's room for much ambiguity. As I have a mildly malicious humour, I'm waiting for the moment when he presses the wrong button. There's little so amusing as seeing a self-acknowledged expert come a cropper.' He crossed to the outside door, opened that, went through.

Alvarez watched as Dale spoke to Lovell. Even at a distance, it was possible to judge from Lovell's expression his sharp annoyance. He took time to close down the laptop, time to come to his feet and walk into the sitting room. He stood with folded arms and stared at a spot above Alvarez's head. 'I said there was no need for an apology.'

Alvarez realized Dale had not explained the reason for this visit – evidence of that slightly malicious humour? 'Señor, I'm sorry to bother you again . . .'

'I am a very busy man, so please say what you have to say.'

'Do you remember telling me you did not have a row with Señor Vickers on Thursday morning?'

Lovell lowered his gaze. 'This has the appearance of a deliberate impertinence!'

'I hope not, señor.'

'It's difficult to imagine how else it might be termed. Or are you incapable of understanding plain English?'

'Sometimes if it is very plain I do find it difficult.'

'One would have hoped otherwise since in the course of your duties you no doubt have to have contact with English nationals of a certain kind.'

'Señor, I need –'

'To understand that the circumstances being what they are, it must be in your interests to leave.'

'I can't until you have answered certain questions.'

'Even allowing for many unfortunate factors, I find your attitude inexplicable.'

'Do you maintain you did not have a row with Señor Vickers on Thursday morning?'

'Of course, since that is the truth. Now you will kindly leave this house.'

'Would you prefer to be questioned at the post?'

'Are you threatening me with arrest?'

'No, señor. Merely trying to point out that it must be far more convenient for you voluntarily to speak to me here than to do so at the post.'

Lovell stood, crossed to the French windows, called out: 'Esme.'

Dale came into the sitting room.

'You're not going to believe this!' Lovell said.

'I will try to suspend my natural instincts.'

'He is threatening to arrest me.'

'A man of considerable talent.'

'It's not a joke.'

'His threat or my perception of it?'

Showing considerable self-control, Lovell spoke calmly. 'He refuses to leave until I answer his impertinent questions. How do I get rid of him?'

'By answering the questions?'

'I have no intention of doing so.'

'Then there would appear to be a problem.'

'Señor,' Alvarez said, 'Señor Dale is correct. If you will just answer me, I will leave immediately.'

'It seems I have to repeat myself ad nauseam. I have no intention of doing that.'

'Surely you would wish to help me uncover the truth?'

'The truth about what?' Dale asked, not trying to hide his curiosity.

'Why the señor continues to say he did not have a row with Señor Vickers on Thursday morning when it is clear that he did.'

'As I have told you, I did not,' Lovell snapped, now openly angry.

'I have spoken to Luisa who confirms the fact.'

'As I told you previously, I am not in the habit of being called a liar by a domestic.'

'Originally, it was Rosa who said you and Señor Vickers

79

had had a row; yesterday, Luisa confirmed that she heard Señor Vickers shouting at you.'

'She is lying.'

'We have a saying: When you lose one sheep, you believe your neighbour, when you lose another, you look for both amongst his flock.'

'This is pure insolence!'

'The question has to be answered, however much it disturbs you.'

Dale said: 'If you'll allow me to interfere, little is easier than to have an argument with Keith since his self-confidence is equalled only by his ignorance. Why should there be significance in the fact that strong words may have passed?'

'There is evidence which suggests Señor Vickers may not have suffered an accident, he may have been murdered.'

Dale whistled.

'That makes no difference,' Lovell said.

'Señor, surely you will understand that this must make a very great difference indeed?'

'Only if one is so irrational as to imagine I could have had anything to do with his death.'

'If he was murdered, the fact that you had a row with him in the morning becomes of the greatest importance until you explain what that row was about . . . I feel certain you will now wish to do that.'

'Your certainty is unfounded.'

'Then I have to ask a further question. Where were you on Thursday evening after seven o'clock?'

'This is becoming farcical.'

'Were you here?'

'Of course.'

Alvarez spoke to Dale. 'And were you and the señora also here?'

'We were –' Dale began, then stopped.

'Señor?'

'I've remembered. Thursday night, we were invited out to dinner; we mentioned to our hostess that we had George staying with us and she said to bring him along, but having

80

previously met her, he decided to stay away. Their politics do not meld.'

Alvarez spoke to Lovell once more. 'You were here all that evening, señor?'

'Yes.'

'On your own?'

'Until my cousin and his wife returned.'

'When was that?'

'I have no idea. I went to bed early.'

'So no one can vouch for you until the following morning?'

'I do not need anyone to vouch for me.'

Had Lovell's manner been less obnoxiously patrician, Alvarez would not have pursued the matter any further at that time, but in a moment of near lunacy, he said: 'Am I correct in believing that you hope to leave the island soon?'

'I fly tomorrow.'

'Then I must ask you not to do so. May I have your word that you will not try to leave?'

'This is intolerable!'

'George,' Dale said, 'a word from on low. Steady on. The police here have very considerable powers.'

'Are you suggesting he can seriously imagine that I could be guilty of murder?'

'The Spanish are a very practical race and so don't award their politicians beatific characters.'

'Snide remarks hardly help the situation.'

'I was merely trying to point out that a more low-key approach might be a good idea. After all, you wouldn't want to make headlines in the UK press, would you, as the first British government minister to be behind bars – that is, at least for the past few months.'

'Are you saying he really can throw me into jail?'

'Since joining the Common Market, the more ridiculous an event, the more likely it is to come to pass.'

'Señor,' Alvarez said, 'if only you will explain what the row with Señor Vickers was about . . .'

'There was no row,' Lovell said furiously. 'How often

81

does one have to say the same thing before it finally filters through?' He calmed down. 'I think you should understand, Inspector, that I shall be taking every permissible measure to register my objection to your behaviour.' He turned, walked with great dignity to the inside doorway, went through.

'Inspector,' Dale said, 'may I pour you a drink?'

CHAPTER 14

The cove was looking enigmatic as well as beautiful. Sharp sunlight and small outcrops of rock created pools of shadow on the hill faces, the faintest of breezes sent ripples across the intensely blue water, a cormorant standing on a rock resembled an elderly relative eagerly awaiting the call to table, hummingbird hawk moths busily worked lantana blossom, a wild goat with heavy horns made the briefest of appearances, cicadas shrilled and then, as if to a conductor's baton, abruptly fell silent . . .

Rosa met Alvarez at the front door and immediately told him that Luisa had just rung to say she would not be in that day because she thought she was starting a bad cold and didn't want to pass it on to anyone else. As if she ever worried about other people! It was Ricardo's day off and so she was skiving, gambling on the fact that the señor wouldn't suddenly turn up . . . He interrupted her to ask if Marti was there.

'He is. Say what you like about him, he's not one who'll stay away just because he likely won't be caught doing it. He's said to me, more than once, "Do a day's work for a day's pay or you have pleased the devil." I wouldn't go along with that, but then his lot see sin everywhere. I always think those kind of people must have very bitter memories hidden away. What do you think?'

'I don't know much about hidden memories.'

'I've never said, of course, but I've often wondered if it was living in a house where everything's forbidden helped to kill his daughter. I mean, if life's all gloom, why try to stay with it? Laughter's the best medicine there is. Pretty as a picture, she was. Needed a life with fun, like you had when you were a lot younger, I'll be bound.'

'It was a hard life.'

'So one found fun more easily.'

'Maybe, maybe not . . . Can you say where I'll find Marti?'

'Doing the pool. At least, that's what he said, when he arrived. I offered him a coffee before starting, but he refused because he's given up drinking it. Yet he really used to like his mugful in the morning. I suppose he's been told coffee's a sin. Would you give up something just because someone says you should?'

'Self-denial is character forming.'

'How would you know?'

He said he'd go and have a word with Marti. She was still talking as he left the kitchen through the outside doorway.

He walked across the downward-sloping lawn to the swimming pool which was in the form of two conjoining circles, the smaller one shallow, the larger one deep enough for a springboard. Marti was hoovering the latter and he looked up at Alvarez's approach, then back down as he slowly continued to move the wheeled suction brush across the bottom.

Even without Rosa's chatter as a guide, Alvarez would have judged Marti to be taciturn, strong-willed or pig-headed depending on definitions, and narrow-minded – the character was there in the lines of the battered face, the set of the mouth, and the way he held his thickset body. He was a survivor from the times of denial, now out of his depths in a consumer world. 'Morning.'

Marti did not bother to acknowledge the greeting.

'I'd like a chat. Enrique Alvarez, Cuerpo General de Policia.'

Marti brought the aluminium handle back and up until he could lay it against the side of the pool, crossed the patio to the complex, on the right-hand side of which was the filter room. He stopped the motor and then, still without a word, returned to the patio and stood, arms at his side, staring out at the cove.

'Shall we sit?' Alvarez suggested.

'Are you tired?'

84

Only a fool or a masochist stood in the sun when he could sit in the shade. He moved back into the large, open, central room of the complex and sat. On his right was a small bar, complete with three shelves laden with bottles. He identified one almost full bottle of Carlos I. Since it seemed unlikely Vickers would be drinking the contents of any of the bottles, he said: 'It's very hot.'

'You expect snow on Puig Major in July?' Marti asked, as he moved to the opposite side of the table.

'One sweats a lot in the heat.'

'If one works.'

'Sweating makes a man very thirsty.'

'There's bottled water in the refrigerator.'

'I always find a little alcohol more effective in stopping thirst than just plain water.'

'The devil always disguises himself.'

Alvarez sighed. When a man believed alcohol to be devilish, he was beyond reason. 'It's five days since Señor Vickers disappeared and there's been no word from him. You may be able to help me work out what might have happened to him.'

Marti was silent.

'When did you leave work on Thursday evening?'

'Same as ever in the summer.'

'Which is when?'

'Eight.'

And never a minute early or a minute late, Alvarez thought. 'D'you know where the señor was when you left here?'

'No.'

'When did you last see him?'

'A while before.'

'How long would a while be?'

'Maybe half an hour.'

'Where was this?'

'On the lawn.' Marti looked up at the gently sloping grass.

'Did you speak to him?'

'He spoke to me.'

85

'What about?'

'Said he wanted me to wash down the decks before he sailed. I told him, it was too near my leaving time.'

'How did he react to that?'

'Same as always when someone won't do as he wants. Starts shouting. Reckons money buys people. Money's the devil's currency.'

Marti's devil seemed to be present everywhere. 'He was angry?'

'Yes.'

'So you quickly washed down the decks?'

'You think I run every time he beckons with his little finger?'

Alvarez was glad that Marti had defied his employer. The true Mallorquin was staunchly and freely independent. 'He accepted your refusal?'

'Said I was to do the decks Friday morning.'

'The next morning?'

'Don't Friday usually come after Thursday?'

Marti could not understand the significance of what he'd just said, any more than Rosa had previously. 'Would you judge the señor had been drinking when he spoke to you?'

'Of course.'

The tone suggested that even one small coñac was cause for bitter reproof. 'Was he on his own?'

'Yes.'

'Do you know when he sailed from here?'

'No.'

'How good was he at handling a boat?'

'How could I judge?'

'You don't know anything about seamanship?'

'And don't want to.'

Alvarez stared out at the cove, the water now glass-still because the breeze had died away. Marti had confirmed or extended some parts of what Rosa and Luisa had told him. Vickers had not set sail before eight, had been on his own, and had perhaps drunk enough to be over-confidently careless. A recipe for accidental disaster. Yet there was the possibility his

86

death had been murder, which meant some of the evidence
had been set to make it look like an accident. How would the
murderer have boarded? By hiding himself before the boat
sailed? But Marti had been around, making that a dangerous
possibility. Much more likely after the *Valhalla* had sailed.
Had he set out in another craft and intercepted the *Valhalla*?
But then why take the dinghy since its absence must be
noticed? Because this reinforced the possibility that Vickers
had used it to check the propeller. But what happened to
the first craft? Sunk? Or had he tricked Vickers into picking
him up from somewhere ashore? Then this must have been
within the confines of the cove because the course to Port
Llueso or beyond would take the *Valhalla* well clear of land
. . . 'Who owns the other side of the cove?'

'The señor.'

'Is there anywhere there the boat could go alongside?'

Marti shrugged his shoulders.

'I need to find out. Can I drive round there?'

'No.'

'Then you'd better show me the way.'

To begin with, the walk was an easy one as it went
across the garden and along the pebble beach; but then it
became a case of climbing rocks, descending rocks, forcing a
way through tangled masses of grass, brambles, weeds, and
between trees whose branches were designed to impale, all
the while being assaulted by squadrons of mosquitoes . . .

Alvarez became convinced that Marti had chosen the most
difficult and dangerous route he could find; the harder the
struggle, the further off the devil was held.

Two-thirds of the way along the cove, an outcrop of bare
rock formed a small natural landing stage. Alvarez looked
down at the water, but it was so clear that depth was virtually
impossible to judge. 'How deep is it here?'

Marti shrugged his shoulders.

Alvarez visually searched for a branch that could be broken
off a tree and used as a sounding rod, but any that was long
enough was too thick. He picked up a stone and dropped it
into the water; just before it reached the bottom, there was

87

a flash of movement which he thought had been caused by a small squid. From the time the stone had taken to fall, he judged the depth of water to be at least two metres – accepting that he could be hopelessly incorrect. 'What's the boat's draught?'

Marti once again shrugged his shoulders.

Alvarez lay down, his head over the edge, and looked for he knew not what. He saw nothing. Grateful to regain his feet – the rock was hard and his stomach larger than he remembered – he began to move and then stopped as, the angle of his view being slightly different, he now saw something. He lay flat once more, reached down, and his forefinger touched something thin and pliable. He gripped this between finger and thumb, freed it from the tiny hook of rock on which it had been caught, and brought it up to eye level. It vaguely resembled a curly brown hair, yet was too thick and rough to be that. He came to his feet, held out the strand. 'Any idea what this is from?'

Marti briefly studied it. 'No.'

Alvarez had a letter which should have been answered a couple of weeks before in the back pocket of his trousers and he put the thread in the envelope. 'OK, let's check the rest of the land.'

The arm of the cove ended abruptly, so abruptly that Alvarez forced his way through a thicket of trees and brambles to find himself out of balance on the edge of a sheer drop which, in his shock, seemed to him to be tens of metres. Panicking, his heart racing and mind threatened with chaos, he threw himself backwards and was stabbed in one leg by the thorn of a large bramble trail. Marti grinned. As Alvarez rubbed the wound, he decided that there were few sins more grievous than gaining amusement from another's misfortune and were it up to him, the penance required would make certain it would be a long time before Marti grinned again.

When Alvarez returned to the kitchen, Rosa said: 'You look real tired!'

'I feel as if I've walked to the moon and back,' he answered as he slumped down on a chair.

'Then you need something to buck you up. A coffee and a coñac?'

'And if your hand slips as you're pouring the coñac, you won't hear me complain.'

She set the coffee machine on the stove, gave him a large brandy and herself a smaller one, sat. 'What have you been doing to get so worn out?'

'Walking to the end of the land on the other side of the cove.'

'Sooner you than me. I tried it once and gave up – it's like a jungle. Why do that in this heat?'

'I wanted to see if the señor could have taken his boat alongside anywhere . . . Which reminds me.' He stood, brought the envelope out from his back pocket and extracted the thread. 'What do you reckon this could be from? It's much too thick to be hair – could it be from some sort of clothing?'

She examined the thread, screwing up her eyes because she should have worn glasses. 'Only if someone's wearing sackcloth and that's unlikely in this day and age. Can't say what it might be, even though . . . Makes me think of something, but I can't think what.'

'No matter.' Even if of no account, as his report to Salas would make plain, he had shown considerable initiative in finding it; especially when he added a description of the perils of the search which had had to be overcome.

They discussed mutual friends who lived in the village. He looked at his watch. 'I'd better return home; it's coming up to lunchtime.'

'You haven't time for another coñac?'

He passed his glass.

She refilled that and her own, added water to hers and ice to both. 'I've just remembered,' she said, as she sat, having passed one glass to him. 'That strand you showed me. I maybe can say what it could have come from.'

'Good.'

'You never can tell with the señor. Occasionally he can

be friendly. One day he asked all three of us if we'd like to go for a trip in his boat – surprised us, I can tell you! Of course, Gaspar said it wasn't a case of being kind, it was the señor boasting, but if Gaspar's a good word for anyone, I've never heard it. And being Gaspar, he refused to go. Probably thought it was a sin. Anyway, we was going alongside somewhere – maybe it was Port Perdia – when the señor shouted to put a fender out. I didn't know what he was on about and we near hit the jetty, only Luisa came along and put the fender out just in time. Strange for her to do something that useful! Of course, the señor was swearing something terrible – not that I could understand the words, but I didn't have to. It wasn't my fault. I just didn't know what he was on about. But for the rest of the trip, he was in one of his bad tempers. Silly to get in that sort of a state, wasn't it?'

'Very silly . . . Was there something about all that which reminds you of the strand I've showed you?'

'The thing is, the fender was made from rope and bits stuck out and as I remember, they was like this.'

He wondered how he could have been so slow.

Twenty minutes later, he was driving along the dirt track to the road, when he suddenly braked to a halt. Assume someone had been on the far arm of the cove, had attracted Vickers's attention and caused him to come alongside the natural landing stage, how had that someone arrived in the area? By walking from Port Llueso? Surely not. Then he (or she) had almost certainly driven there, but would have needed to hide the car. The dirt track was narrow, the scrub dense, but he'd just passed a small clearing on the left-hand side.

He left the car and walked back along the track – sweating, breathless, and quickly regretting this latest display of initiative – to reach a clearing larger than he had expected because it curved round in a rough arc; a car could easily be placed out of sight of the track. A brief search found a piece of paper caught up on a bramble trail. He smoothed this out and because there had been no rain in weeks, there was no difficulty in identifying a bill for two people who had eaten at Restaurante Monserrat, in Runyman, on the fourteenth of June. Runyman was very near to where Señora Vickers lived.

CHAPTER 15

As Alvarez entered the dining room, Jaime looked at him over the rim of the glass from which he had been about to drink. 'You're late and she's fussing.' Jaime nodded in the direction of the bead curtain. 'Keeps looking in to see if you're back and saying that if you don't hurry up, the meal will be ruined.'

'Is it something special?'

Jaime drank. 'All I know is, she started blaming me for you being late. I told her not to be so bloody silly.'

'In those exact words?'

'Well, sort of.'

Very sort of, Alvarez thought as he reached across to the sideboard for a glass.

The bead curtain parted as Dolores stepped through it. 'You have decided to come back, then?' she said, as the strings of plastic beads slowly stopped clashing into each other.

'I've been working flat out and couldn't get away until the very last moment.'

'I will try very hard to believe that.' She returned into the kitchen, causing the bead curtain to clash noisily again for a few seconds.

Alvarez drank. 'What I said is the truth.'

'In her present mood, she wouldn't believe Ananias.'

He looked at Jaime.

'What's up with you?'

'Ananias lied about something and dropped down dead.'

Jaime drained his glass. 'So what? And if that happened these days, there wouldn't be anyone left alive.'

Dolores returned to the room. 'Are you ready to eat or do you want still more time in which to befuddle yourselves?'

'It's been medically proven that alcohol is good for one,' Alvarez said defensively.

'Only when drunk in moderation, a possibility that has never occurred to either of you . . . Your superior chief has rung twice; he says you are to phone him the moment you return.'

'I wonder what's up with him?'

'He complained that you haven't been at the post.' She sniffed loudly. 'But you tell me you have been working hard. Perhaps at improving your Italian?'

'At forcing a way through near-impenetrable jungle.'

'And no doubt fighting a ten-metre anaconda?'

He drained his glass and was about to refill it when a sense of caution stayed his hand.

'Even for a Madrileño,' she said, 'Señor Salas's manner was curt and rude.'

'It always is.'

'Were I in your position, I would long since have asked him to try to show some manners.' She returned to the kitchen.

'You know something,' Alvarez said in a low voice, 'I believe she really would.'

'If you ask me –' Jaime hastily stopped as she returned.

Protected by oven gloves, she was carrying an earthenware pot. 'Would one of you set a tile on the table so I can put this down, or will that disturb your drinking?'

Jaime, nearer to the several tiles with felt bases on top of the sideboard, reached out for one and placed this on the table.

As she settled the pot on the tile, she said: 'Have you rung the superior chief?'

'He's probably at lunch so I'll do it later on,' Alvarez replied.

'If women were like men, beds would not be made, meals would not be cooked, houses would not be cleaned.'

If women were like men, he thought, the world would be a more restful place.

*   *   *

94

The distant ringing of the telephone awoke him. To his surprise, there was no immediate response. Then he heard Dolores hurrying past the door and he relaxed and welcomed back sleep . . .

'Enrique, it's for you,' she called out from downstairs.

He slowly dragged himself into a sitting position on the bed and stared at the far wall. A loud bang on the door startled him.

'It's your ill-mannered superior chief.'

Even for Salas, it was an extraordinary thing to do – to ring in the middle of siesta time. Then he checked what the time was and saw it was after five o'clock. In sleep or a woman's arms, an hour was but a minute . . .

Salas was at his most abrupt. 'I have learned that, as unbelievable as this might seem, you have again insulted Señor Lovell.'

'No, señor –'

'Do you deny that you have questioned him once more?'

'That was because I learned –'

'I suggest you have managed to go through life without learning anything. In typical gentlemanly fashion, Señor Lovell apologized for again raising the matter; he expressed the sincere hope that what he said would be accepted in the friendly and understanding fashion in which it was given. But despite the duty a guest owes his host country to acquiesce in the laws and customs of that country, he regretfully felt obliged to express his embarrassed annoyance at being called a murderer. Some things are said to be inconceivable. Would that this were true. Yet who, this side of bedlam, could have imagined that a mere inspector would call an important member of the British government a murderer?'

'Señor, I did not do so. It was he who said that that was what I was saying, because I had said –'

'Did you tell Señor Lovell there was evidence to suggest Señor Vickers might not have drowned accidentally?'

'Yes, but –'

'Did you demand Señor Lovell provided an alibi for the presumed time of death?'

'Yes, but –'

95

'And when he did so, did you refuse to believe him?'

'Because he kept lying about the row with Señor Vickers. I asked him several times to tell the truth so there would be no need for any further action . . .'

'He has repeatedly assured you there was no such row.'

'But Rosa told me –'

'Even a moment's thought would have suggested she must either be exaggerating or lying.'

'Luisa corroborates what she said.'

'Who?'

'Luisa. She also works at Ca'n Mortice and she heard Señor Vickers shouting at Señor Lovell.'

There was a silence.

'Señor, however much one wishes to respect the word of an Englishman, it is surely necessary to remember Señor Lovell is a politician. And with Rosa's evidence fully corroborated, I decided it must be right to doubt that the señor was telling me the truth. That caused me to ask, why should he be lying? As yet, there can be no ready answer, but the reason surely has to be a strong one since it will be obvious that to risk being seen to be lying about matters concerning the disappearance of Señor Vickers must be to raise suspicions.'

'Have you determined whether someone close to Vickers is the beneficiary of a very large insurance policy on his life; whether he has large debts; whether such debts may have been incurred in an illegal practice which renders him liable to extreme physical abuse if he does not pay?'

'No, señor.'

'Why not?'

'Because it didn't seem worth doing.'

'You place your judgement above my orders?'

'If he was murdered, there can be no question of his faking his own death.'

'To assume something without the facts to support it, to carry out an investigation on the basis of that assumption while ignoring all other possibilities, is a sign of blinkered incompetence.'

'But surely the coñac, rope fibre and restaurant bill, when

considered together, so point to the probability of murder that such an assumption is justified?'

'What are you talking about?'

Alvarez explained.

'Why have I not been informed of these facts?'

'There hasn't been time . . .'

'An efficient detective makes time . . . It clearly has not occurred to you that if a man suddenly gives up drinking coñac, he may with equal suddenness resume drinking it; that there is nothing to identify the fibre as having come from a rope fender or that if it did, then that fender was put out from the señor's yacht on Thursday evening; that the restaurant bill does no more than show two people ate a meal there last month.'

'Each fact on its own is capable of an innocuous explanation, but put them all together and it's difficult to ignore their combined weight.'

'That entirely depends on who is doing the weighing.'

'Señora Vickers lives near Runyman.'

'Which leads you to what conclusion?'

'The obvious one – that she was at some time in a car in the clearing where I found the bill. What was she doing there? Spying out the land, making certain a car could be parked out of sight, that she would be able to get to the spot on the cove where there is a natural landing place?'

'You are suggesting Señora Vickers murdered her husband?'

'Much more likely, he was murdered by her and her boyfriend together.'

'You accuse a notable member of the British government. Next, Señor Vickers's wife, whom you naturally assume is committing adultery since you cannot forego thoughts of a salacious nature. Who will be your next suspect? A member of the British royal family? . . . Unfortunately, due to severe staff shortages I cannot immediately send someone to Llueso to take over your duties, in particular, the investigation into Vickers's disappearance, so regrettably you cannot be immediately replaced, but until you are, you will on no account, on no account whatsoever, carry out any further inquiries into the Vickers case. Is that totally and absolutely clear?'

'Señor, what I've done –'

'Has been to exhibit an astonishing degree of incompetence, not to mention an inexcusable refusal to obey orders.' Salas cut the connection.

A man could only do his best, Alvarez thought. But then, of course, it was that which Salas considered to be the problem.

CHAPTER 16

Alvarez, slumped in the chair in his office, stared unseeingly at the shuttered window. Would he be dismissed from the Cuerpo? Salas would surely call for this, and the adjudicators at the hearing were bound to be elderly officers whose standards would be harsh and sympathies slight because the dignity of seniority needed to be upheld . . .

Retirement was certainly to be welcomed, but not the loss of pension if this was through dismissal. In the old days, a man could live cheaply and be content, but that no longer seemed possible; an agricultural community had become a consumer society with ever-rising standards. Once, one had taken an empty bottle along to the nearest bodega and for a few pesetas it had been filled with coñac from a barrel; now, coñac could not be sold from a barrel and the cheapest bottle cost nearly a thousand pesetas, more if the tourist trade was strong.

If he were unable to pay his share of housekeeping, there would never be the slightest possibility of Jaime and Dolores asking him to leave. Unlike the modern generation, they held family ties to be sacrosanct. But he could not become a financial burden to them, so he would have to find a job. At what? In the tourist trade? It would be very difficult to learn to return drunken abuse with polite helpfulness. In the building trade? There was little room for out-of-condition labourers and he had no carpentering or plumbing skills . . .

The phone interrupted his dismal thoughts.

'Enrique, you said you wanted to be told the moment a body turned up. Carlos Ibañez has just come into port and says one has been washed up in a small cove almost at the point of Cap Parelona, on the southern side.'

'Could it be that of Señor Vickers?'

'One minute.'

There was a short silence.

'He says it's impossible to judge anything much beyond the fact that it's male.'

'Can I get down to the cove from the road?'

Another pause.

'It's possible, but difficult unless you're good at rock climbing.'

'Tell him he'll have to take me there in his boat.'

'Hang on . . . He says he's far too busy and you'll have to find someone else.'

'Does he want me to start checking if he found the body because the cove is being used for smuggling?'

Alvarez could just hear the flow of invective when that message was relayed.

He had never known the call of the sea. Not for him a nostalgic vision of square-riggers with acres of billowing canvas, mastheads circling the sky to the movements of hulls, the threshing of blocks and tackles, of sheets and halyards, the kick of the wheel, yet he found a pleasure difficult to classify in skimming across the blue water, rent in white by their wake, with stark cliffs to port and endless sea to starboard; the pleasure undimmed by the sour suspicion of Ibañez, who clearly couldn't decide whether he was believed when he swore by all that he held holy that he'd never smuggled so much as a single cigarette in his life.

The cove was not readily identifiable as such because the irregular rock faces confused the very narrow entrance; as a further defence against interfering authority, there were underwater rocks that would tear the bottom out of any boat that struck them. Ibañez steered past them with a skill that spoke of great familiarity, cut the engine; they drifted up to the pebbled shoreline.

He pointed. The bundle at the water's edge had no shape so that it was not immediately apparent that it was a body.

Alvarez tried not to show his reluctance to do what must be done as he scrambled over the side of the boat. Death always shocked him, even when it had been kind, because it reminded him all too sharply of his own mortality. He crossed the pebbles to the corpse. This lay on its side, one arm outstretched. He hunkered down in order to examine the face more closely. Allowing for the distortions, he judged the man to be of the same age and description as Vickers. The clothes were strangely formal for the height of summer – shirt and tie, grey linen trousers, socks, black shoes. Vickers hoping that sartorial smartness really did help seduction? A glint on one of the fingers of the outstretched hand caught his attention – a signet ring. A strand of seaweed had become caught up on it and he pulled this free to see the entwined letters KAV.

He stood. 'Is there any risk of this being washed out to sea?'

'You think there'll be a three-metre tide to sail it to Menorca?'

'Then you can run me back to the port to find the photographer and the doctor.'

Ibañez clearly would have liked to tell Alvarez to walk.

The doctor, one of two in the area who were qualified to do forensic work, left the body and crossed to where Alvarez stood. 'There are two wounds, one in the head and one in the stomach, but judging by the signs, the cause of death was drowning – the postmortem, of course, will confirm that. The blow to the back of the head was delivered by some kind of blunt instrument and probably knocked him unconscious; there are signs that a rope or cord was tied to one ankle and this obviously suggests he was secured to a weight to keep the body hidden underwater, but the knots were inexpertly tied and became undone.'

So it was murder. It would have been a total waste of time to have investigated the possibility of a faked death as the superior chief had so insistently demanded he did. But experience suggested that when he received the report,

Salas would maintain he had always considered murder more likely . . . 'What about the wound to the stomach?'

'It's probably deep, but I can't say what sort of internal damage it inflicted. Judging by the entry, the weapon used was of considerable width. What it could have been, I've no idea. Any more than why the injury was inflicted when the blow to the head must have incapacitated the victim.'

'Perhaps it came first?'

'Had it done, surely there would have been no need for the blow to the head?' The doctor drew on his cigarette, dropped the stub on to the pebbles. 'I accept that it is a mistake to speculate beyond the facts as presented, but I see it as an injury inflicted either by a mind in shambles or consumed by a wild hatred.'

Alvarez thought that if there were such hatred in the world, could any man be safe?

The photographer, two cameras strung around his neck and a bag in his right hand, came across to where they stood. 'I've taken all the shots you asked for.'

'Thanks,' Alvarez said.

The doctor looked at his watch. 'I need to get back. Inspector, you'll arrange for the body to be taken to the morgue, won't you?' It had been more a command than a question.

When Alvarez arrived home, the family had finished the main course and were eating bananas and baked almonds.

'You're very late,' Dolores said challengingly.

'I'm sorry,' he replied meekly. 'A body was washed ashore in a cove near the tip of Cap Parelona and I had to go and view it, return to collect the doctor and photographer, and then arrange for it to be collected.'

'Was it all bleeding?' Juan asked with excited interest.

'Enough of that!' Dolores snapped. 'I will not have such talk in this house.'

'Uncle said —'

'Since I am attempting to bring you up to live a decent life, you will ignore much of what both your father and uncle say.' She turned her head to face Alvarez. 'Is it too much

102

to ask you not to speak about such things in front of the children?'

'I didn't say anything about blood. Anyway, they hear and see much worse on television . . .'

'You find that an excuse for your crudity? Ayee! Could life be harder than trying to raise two children to lead a worthwhile life when they are constantly subjected to such harmful influences?' She stood. 'I will get your meal, Enrique, which I have kept warm, but it will have been ruined. That is not my fault, but no doubt I will be blamed.' She swept out of the kitchen.

Alvarez reached across for the bottle of brandy that was at the end of the table, poured himself a drink. It was astonishing how a whirlwind could descend out of clear air . . .

Juan looked at the bead curtain, then leaned across the table. 'Uncle, was the body all in little bits?'

'No.'

'Rafael's got a video game in which, if you get it right, you splat the other fighter to pieces.'

'If I were you, I would not mention that fact to your mother.'

Dolores returned, a plate in her hand.

'Juan has a game . . .' Isabel began, then gave a yelp. 'He kicked me!'

Dolores put the plate down in front of Alvarez. 'Why did you kick your sister?' she asked Juan.

'I didn't.'

'Yes, he did,' Isabel said.

'What game have you bought that I wouldn't like to hear about?'

'I haven't bought any 'cause I've no money.'

'Then what game have you borrowed?'

'None.' Juan stared intently at Isabel, promising her endless harassment if she said anything. There a deep silence.

'There are times when I can only despair!' Dolores sat. She picked up an almond and ate it.

Alvarez finished the brandy, refilled his glass with wine.

He ate a mouthful of tumbet. 'This hasn't begun to spoil, not even by a little. It's delicious.'

'Why do men think women so credulous they will believe their stupid lies?' she asked sadly.

Because to tell the truth – that the dish would have disgraced even an English kitchen – would have caused ten times as much trouble.

When he finished his meal, he said: 'I have to go out.' He stood.

'Before your siesta?' Dolores asked, her tone sharp.

'It's urgent work that can't wait.'

'Naturally.'

'That's fact.'

'Isabel,' she said to her daughter, 'you are young, yet sadly old enough to have to learn that when a man tells you something is fact, you can be certain it is fiction.'

'Why won't you . . . ?' Alvarez began, then became silent. It had to be admitted that she had some cause for surprise. He could not remember when he had last foregone his siesta, but really he'd no choice in the matter. Lovell was flying back to England early that evening and would be leaving for the airport in the middle of the afternoon.

He left the house and walked along the pavement to his car, unlocked the driving door and settled behind the wheel. The interior was like an oven, even though he'd left all four windows slightly open. That mythical win in the lottery would first buy him a car with air-conditioning . . .

He drove across the bridge and then along the old road to Cala Roig. Years ago, every field he passed would have been carefully cultivated, every caseta a primitive home or 'summer residence'. Now, few of the fields bore crops, every caseta had been modernized and enlarged and five new houses had been built, all with swimming pools because they were let to tourists. The land was being prostituted.

He parked in front of Ca Na Atalla. Dale, dressed in T-shirt and shorts, opened the front door. 'This is unexpected, but can I call it an unexpected pleasure?'

'I hope I am not interrupting your lunch, señor?'

'We are sitting back and enjoying its memories.'

'I should like to speak with Señor Lovell, if I may.'

Dale stepped out on to the porch, closed the door behind him. 'Inspector, a masochist has been defined as someone who interferes in an argument that doesn't concern him. Despite that, I'm going to take the risk. Obviously I don't know what you intend to say to my cousin, but inevitably, and however politely put, your words will arouse fresh resentment and result in his complaining yet again to authority . . . So what I'm saying in a long-winded manner is, are you quite certain it is advisable to speak to him now? When he's about to return home?'

'I think so, señor.'

'You cannot leave the problem to time? There's no better solvent.'

'Unfortunately not.'

'A pity. Then, as Hollywood has taught us, a man has to do what a man has to do.' He turned round, opened the front door, gestured Alvarez inside with a brief wave of his right hand.

The meal had been eaten out on the patio, and side plates, cheese dish, and four bottles of liqueurs, remained on the table.

'Hullo, Inspector,' Geraldine said, as Alvarez stepped out of the house.

Lovell did not speak, but his expression suggested several four-letter words.

'I apologize for interrupting you,' Alvarez said formally.

'There's no need,' Geraldine replied. 'Do sit down. And will you have a liqueur – Cointreau, Benedictine, green chartreuse, or hierbas?'

'A small hierbas would be delicious, señora.'

'I'll get a glass.' Dale went indoors.

'Why are you here?' Lovell asked bluntly.

'George, why not let the poor man relax and enjoy his drink first?' Geraldine suggested.

Lovell ignored her. 'Well – what's the answer?'

'I have to ask you something, señor,' Alvarez replied.

'Do you know what this would be called in England? Police persecution.'

'I hope, señor, you do not think I have been persecuting you?'

'Can you suggest another name for hounding me without even the shadow of a valid reason for doing so?'

'George . . .' Geraldine began.

'I'm sorry, Geraldine, but you must leave me to handle this matter.'

When Dale returned, she looked up at him and, certain Lovell could not see her face, made an expression of resigned hopelessness.

Lovell spoke to Alvarez. 'Your conduct has now gone beyond all reason.'

Dale picked up the bottle of hierbas and began to pour. 'In the late nineteenth century, a traveller to this island wrote in a largely unreadable guidebook that of all the island's charms, the lack of rational reason was the greatest.'

Lovell said curtly, 'That sort of comment is hardly helpful.'

'The truth seldom is.' He handed the glass to Alvarez.

'Señor,' Alvarez said, 'it has become even more in your interest to answer my questions.'

Lovell was at his most pompous. 'As I remember having previously said, it is I, not you, who will decide where my interests lie.'

'I must ask again, what was the subject of the row between you and Señor Vickers last Thursday morning?'

'How often does one have to repeat something before it is finally understood? There was no row.'

'I need to know because Señor Vickers sailed from his home that evening and disappeared and –'

'There is a point at which repetition becomes highly offensive.'

'Surely you can understand that the subject of any row the señor had must be of very great importance all the time this is unknown? Whereas, once known, it will probably be seen to be of no account whatsoever . . .'

'There is no point in continuing this conversation.'

'You are due to fly to England very shortly?'

'And if I am?'

'I must ask you to delay your departure.'

'I have told you before, I will do no such thing.'

'This morning, a body was discovered after it had been washed ashore. It has yet to be confirmed the dead man is Señor Vickers, but there can be little doubt. He was murdered.'

'My God!' Geraldine said, her voice high. She spoke very quickly. 'Until now, I was so certain that however things looked, he'd just taken off after some woman who'd caught his attention. But murdered! On this Island of Calm!'

'"The canker of a calm world and a long peace",' Dale quoted.

Lovell judged that even in the face of so small and unprofitable an audience he should provide a conventional response. 'Shocking news; truly shocking! Death is always sad, but when it comes in the guise of violence, it is barbarically tragic. It is to be hoped, Inspector, that you very soon identify the guilty party.'

'Indeed, señor. And I am sure you can now understand why I have to continue my investigations.'

'Of course.'

'So perhaps you will finally explain what your row with Señor Vickers was about?'

Lovell's manner changed. 'I have answered that question, many, many times.'

'In fact, señor, you have not answered it.'

'I will say it once more. There was no row.'

'Then you leave me with no option other than to ask you for your passport.'

'What?'

'Señor, the subject of the row has potentially become of the greatest importance, yet even though I am certain you understand this, you still refuse to explain it. You will not voluntarily delay your departure, so I must make certain that you do not leave the island before I give you permission to do so.'

'I have never before heard such ridiculous nonsense. Are you suffering from some mental incapacity?'

'There are some who may well think so. Nevertheless, you must hand me your passport.'

'I shall do no such thing.'

'Then I will have to ask a member of the Guardia to help me collect it.'

'I . . . I cannot believe this. A member of the British government being treated like some common criminal!'

For a moment no one spoke. From a nearby wild olive tree there suddenly came the jewelled song of a nightingale, apparently ignorant of the time of day.

Dale finally broke the silence. 'George, I strongly advise you to hand the inspector your passport. Then everything can be sorted out quietly.'

'This is unbelievable!'

'The more unbelievable, the more the media will revel in the circumstances the moment they learn about them.'

Anger thickened Lovell's voice. 'You will regret this,' he said to Alvarez.

'Señor, I can only do my duty.'

He stood, kicked his chair back with an angry sweep of the leg, strode across the patio and into the house.

'You are a persistent man,' Dale said.

'For many generations, señor, the people of this island had only their stubbornness to keep them alive.'

CHAPTER 17

The brave man, not knowing fear, died; the coward suffered fear in all its guises, but lived; the prevaricator couldn't decide whether to live or to die. Alvarez sat at his desk and ransacked his mind for a reason not to phone the superior chief. He failed. He lifted the receiver and dialled Palma.

'Yes?' said the secretary, with all the curtness of assumed authority.

He told her he wished to speak to the superior chief.

'Yes?' said Salas, with all the curtness of authority.

He decided to put things in an illogical order to draw, and therefore diffuse, Salas's wrath early on. 'Señor, I should like to report that earlier this afternoon I went to Señor Dale's house and spoke to Señor Lovell. Since he continued to refuse to cooperate, I confiscated his passport to make certain he cannot return to England until given permission to do so.'

There was a long silence. Finally, Salas said: 'I'm damned if I know what to say!' He then contradicted himself and in many words implied that Alvarez was qualified to do little more than pedal an ice-cream tricycle around the tourist beaches, if, of course, that was not too considerable a drain on his abilities . . . 'What was the last order I gave you?'

'That I was not to carry out any further investigation into the disappearance of Señor Vickers.'

'So, in your inimitable style, you immediately confiscate the señor's passport! I have in the past suggested you consult a psychiatrist. I should have ordered you to do so since then you would have been declared unfit to remain in the Cuerpo and the present catastrophe could never have arisen . . . What do I say to the Director General? How do I persuade him that any officer can be so bereft of intelligence that when given an order, he immediately disobeys it?'

'Señor . . .'

'I shall, of course, again explain you were appointed before I took command . . .'

'Señor . . .'

'Don't interrupt.'

'But I think you should know that Señor Vickers's body was found this morning in a small cove by Cap Parelona. The preliminary judgement is that he drowned after receiving a heavy blow to the head and a deep wound to his stomach; it seems probable a weight was attached to a leg to hold his body underwater, but the knot unravelled. In these circumstances, I judged that Señor Lovell's row with Señor Vickers –'

'If there was one,' Salas interrupted weakly.

'I find it more difficult to doubt Rosa's and Luisa's evidence than to believe Señor Lovell's.' He waited, but when the other remained silent, he continued: 'That row becomes of the very greatest importance until and unless an explanation proves it obviously had nothing to do with the murder. Knowing that Señor Lovell was due to fly from the island early this evening, I deemed it essential to delay his departure.'

'You should have realized that a man in his position cannot be treated so cavalierly and so should have detailed what had happened and then very politely asked him to explain the row.'

'I did, but he continued to deny there had been one.'

'Then you should have asked him on his word as an English gentleman not to leave the island until the matter is cleared up.'

'If he is an English gentleman, he cannot be lying, can he? – but he is. Nevertheless, I did ask for his assurance that he would not fly off; he refused to give that. I was left with no option other than to confiscate his passport.'

'Goddamnit, Alvarez, why is it that whenever you become involved in a case, it becomes impossibly confused?'

'It's not my fault –'

'Why else would you be so quick to try to exculpate yourself? What do you intend to do now?'

'If Señor Lovell continues to refuse to say what the row was about, I must try and discover the truth by other means.'

'Such as?'

'An investigation into Señor Vickers's financial affairs might offer a clue.'

'I suggested that a long time ago.'

'Indeed, señor, but for a different reason. Now, we need to know if Señora Vickers had reason for wishing her husband dead – perhaps she is the main beneficiary under his will. Then, although I wouldn't suggest a financial connection, Señorita Lockwood –'

'Who?'

'The señorita he was due to meet on the Thursday evening.'

'Why is she a suspect?'

'Rather than a suspect, someone who might be able to suggest a line of investigation. But, in truth, it is possible to conceive she could have had a motive for his murder.'

'What?'

'If Rosa's judgement is accepted, she was initially trying to keep the señor at arm's-length to increase his ardour; perhaps he became so inflamed, he raped her and instead of reporting the incident, she determined to gain her own revenge.'

'Even de Sade would be appalled by your mind.'

'Such things happen, señor.'

'But, thank God, only the depraved go out of their way to invent them . . . Did the blow to Vickers's head kill him?'

'The doctor, as always, wasn't prepared to be definite at this stage, but doesn't have much doubt he died from drowning. We'll have to wait for the postmortem result for confirmation.'

'You will keep me informed of every step of your investigation – is that perfectly clear?'

'I am to continue?'

'What the devil do you mean?'

'You said you were replacing me.'

'When that was possible. At the moment it remains impossible. I can only hope that the delay will not lead to a further escalation of depravity.' Salas cut the connection.

Alvarez leaned back in his chair, enjoying the cooling draught of the fan. By careful manipulation, he had avoided the scathing condemnation he might have expected. A successful life was all about knowing how to avoid the worst.

Puerta Playa Neuva had once been no more than a small commercial and even smaller fishing port and a many-kilometres-long pristine sandy beach; now, it was a busy commercial port, an almost moribund fishing port, and a kilometres-long beach that was engulfed by bathers and their litter and backed by downmarket holiday apartments and bungalows, supermarkets, shops selling tourist trash, cafés fuelling the lager louts, and restaurants serving meals like mum makes. However, away from this bedlam there was open land and on the hills there were properties from which one could look out above the mess to the sea and still see beauty.

Ca'n Arboles – a number of pines surrounded the property – was a large, one-floor house with a hint of elegance which suggested the architect had been a foreigner. Built halfway up a hill, where the land was briefly almost level, it offered an uninterrupted view of the whole of Playa Neuva Bay. Having rung the bell, Alvarez turned and stared out to sea. Considerably larger than Llueso Bay, it lacked the backing mountains which made Llueso Bay so complete and perfect . . .

The front door, elaborately patterned in a dark wood, was opened by a young woman wearing a maid's apron over a brightly coloured frock. He introduced himself, asked if Señora Vickers was at home. She led the way through the house to the patio, in the centre of which was a circular pool. By the side of the pool, a middle-aged woman still able to wear a bikini with credibility, was lying face downwards on a lilo; in the pool, a man many years younger than she, was swimming with a stylish crawl.

'Inspector Alvarez, Cuerpo General de Policia,' announced the maid, her tone slightly dramatic.

The swimmer came to a stop and stood, water just below his bronzed shoulders, and stared at Alvarez. Laura Vickers turned over and moved into a sitting position. The years had lined and slightly thickened her face, yet there was no missing the fact that she had been beautiful when young.

'Good evening, señora,' Alvarez said, in English. 'I apologize for interrupting your evening, but I need to speak with you.'

'Are you a detective?'

'Yes.'

'You're here because of my husband?'

'That is so.'

She came to her feet with the ease of someone physically fit. 'Let's move into the shade.' She began to walk towards the patio, whose roof consisted of rush matting set on metal supports, stopped as Serra called out from the pool.

'What is the problem?' he asked in fluent, but heavily accented English.

'The inspector wants to talk about Keith, that's all.'

'Why?'

'I don't yet know.'

'Perhaps I will be with you.'

'You stay where you are, pet.'

'But –'

'Just stay.'

It had almost been a command, Alvarez thought. Her manner reinforced the impression he had gained over the phone – a strong character.

She resumed walking, to come to a stop by a round patio table in the shade. She sat, took off the reflective sunglasses she had been wearing and, as he settled opposite her, said: 'Presumably, you're here because you've some news of Keith?'

'Yes, señora.'

'What is it?'

113

To pass on bad news could be the most emotionally demanding job of a policeman, yet he had every reason to be sure there would be little anguish. Still, the conventions needed to be observed. 'Señora, I am very sorry to have to tell you that a body was found this morning washed up in a cove on Cap Parelona and there is reason to believe it may be that of your husband.'

'You aren't certain?'

'A formal identification hasn't yet been possible. But I have something to show you and to ask if you recognize it.'

'What?'

He brought a matchbox out of his pocket; inside was the signet ring from the dead man's finger, wrapped in cotton wool. He handed her this.

She stared at it for several seconds. 'That's his.'

'You can be certain?'

'When we became engaged, I asked him what I could give him as an engagement present and he said a signet ring. I bought this and had it engraved with his initials. He was annoyed I'd had the A included because he hated the name Albert, but would never say why. My guess is he considered it common. Rather ironic, wouldn't you say?'

He carefully did not answer. 'May I have it back, señora; for the moment it must remain in the police's possession.' He returned it to the matchbox. 'It will be necessary to have a visual identification for final confirmation that the ring wasn't being worn by someone else.'

'How could that possibly happen?'

'Señora, we always have to eliminate the possibilities, however improbable,' he answered, unwilling to suggest the possibility of a faked death. 'I may have to ask you to view the body, but I hope that won't be necessary and one of the staff at Ca'n Mortice will be able to do this.'

'I'd rather that: I'm a coward when it comes to death.' She began to fiddle with her dark glasses. 'What happened? Did he accidentally fall over the side of the boat and drown?'

Little evidence of sorrow, but then she would have had to

114

be a masterful hypocrite to have burst into tears when her toy boy was in the swimming pool, trying to hear what they were saying. 'Not exactly, señora.'

'What does that mean?'

'He suffered a very heavy blow to the back of his head which probably knocked him unconscious before he drowned, and also a wound to the stomach.'

'Are you saying he was murdered?'

'I'm afraid so.'

She stared into space. 'That's funny.'

'Funny, señora?'

She looked directly at him. 'Inspector, there's no call to look shocked and outraged. Blame the English language which often uses a word in two opposite meanings. I mean funny strange, not funny humorous. Keith was always scared that someone would try to kill him.'

'Why should he have thought that?'

'Probably because he'd swindled so many people, he reckoned sooner or later one of them would try to get his own back.'

'Swindled?'

'If you like euphemisms, call it bested in business. He made his fortune in property development; no one's ever managed to do that and remain whiter than white.'

'Can you suggest the name of anyone who might have had reason to dislike him very much?'

'He never discussed business with me, probably because he thought that if he did so, I might gain a doubtful image of him. My husband . . . my late husband, had the typical desire of the weak man to be liked even when he'd given cause to be thoroughly disliked.'

'You would call him a weak man?'

'The strong man doesn't give a damn what someone else thinks of him.'

There was a call from the pool. 'Is there much trouble?'

'Nothing you need bother about.'

'I think I shall be with you.'

'No, pet. The inspector and I are getting on very well.'

When certain Serra was doing as she'd said, she turned back to Alvarez: 'He's a charming man.'

That was not the adjective he would have used.

She had not missed his disapproval. 'Marcos and I have a perfect relationship,' she said aggressively.

'I'm glad to hear that.'

'Liar!'

'Señora . . .'

'When a man of forty beds a woman of twenty, great; when a woman of forty beds a man of twenty, tacky. Isn't that your reaction?'

'For me, a relationship which brings happiness is to be envied, whatever the ages.'

She studied him. 'You know, you sounded sincere when you said that!'

'I was.'

'What an odd detective you are beginning to appear to be.'

'In what sense do you use the word "odd"?'

She laughed, her white teeth in sharp contrast to her bronzed face. 'Purely complimentary . . . Tell me something. Would you call yourself a typical Mallorquin?'

'Yes.'

'How very definite! Then you must be thirsty as it's after six o'clock. What would you like to drink?'

'A small coñac would be very welcome.'

She stood, walked round the table and past him to go into the house.

She might be forty as she'd indicated, or even a little more allowing for female forgetfulness, but maturity had given depth to her attractions . . . He swore. She was a woman who openly disgraced herself by having a relationship with a very much younger man – there were limits to his enlightened tolerance, whatever he'd said to her – and yet he was having lustful thoughts. Would he ever grow old enough to look at an attractive woman without images of sex sneaking into his mind . . . ?

Laura returned and said: 'Francisca will bring the drinks out.'

'Señora, how long were you married to your husband?'

'Too long.' She stared challengingly at him. 'Have I finally shocked you?'

'Of course not.'

'Again, liar! How you men try to look down on us. If a man has an unhappy marriage, he can tell the world about it; if a woman does, she must coyly whisper that things didn't work out, probably because of her own fault. When I married I was, even though I say it myself, bloody attractive. But that did not stop Keith chasing after every woman who couldn't or wouldn't run fast enough. The first time I learned he'd been grazing in other pastures, we'd been married for precisely two months. He apologized with a diamond necklace and sealed his promise never to do such a thing again with a luxury cruise.

'When I finally had the gumption to understand he was led by his penis, I wanted to divorce him. Only . . . I realized he'd outsmarted me. He knew I'd already become so used to luxury that I wouldn't be able to face the prospect of returning to a life in which every single pound had to be stretched. If I divorced him, he'd be vindictive enough to make certain any divorce settlement was little more than peanuts – most of his capital was offshore and very well hidden from the taxman. So I remained Mrs Laura Vickers and every time he looked at a woman – as he grew older, his tastes became younger – I carefully stared the other way. That continued when we came out here to live, except for a short while when it seemed he could meet a receptive bimbo without stamping his feet and snorting. For a while, we almost had a marriage. Then he met a blonde at a cocktail party . . . Or was she the redhead that had him gasping like a stranded trout? . . . and it was back to normal.'

Francisca came out on to the patio, tray in hand. She placed two glasses and an earthenware bowl containing crisps on the table, walked out to the edge of the pool and put a third glass down. 'Señor Serra, your drink,' she said in Mallorquin.

Alvarez thought he heard a note of contempt in her voice. She returned past them to go into the house.

'Life's for ever playing jokes,' Laura said as she raised her glass.

He wondered what that meant. 'When did you separate from the señor?'

'Does that really matter?'

'I need to find out all I can about him.'

'Not worth the effort.'

'He has been murdered, señora.'

'And you think I'm an unfeeling bitch.'

'Of course not.'

'As a man, you won't understand or be able to appreciate the depth of the humiliation I felt.'

A humiliation for which she was now gaining revenge? 'Was the separation recent?'

'Last year.'

'At your suggestion?'

'At his.'

'What reason did he give?'

'Something stupid along the lines that we should each have the chance to lead our own life – I don't really remember. It was all too obvious that he'd decided to remove me temporarily in order to judge whether to do so permanently. I would have told him to go to hell, but he offered me a very large allowance because, so he said, he realized how I'd provided him with a nice home – what he meant was, a respectable public front behind which he could play the private part of a randy old goat. But hearing him, I demanded that the settlement was drawn up by lawyers – he agreed.'

'Did you meet him after your separation?'

'Once only.'

'Who suggested this meeting.'

'He did.'

'Did he say why?'

'I kept waiting for some sanctimonious explanation, but there just wasn't one. I confess that had me wondering whether he was regretting the separation.'

118

For some reason, more intuitive than logical, her 'confession' made him think that now she was lying. 'Do you know if he made a Spanish will?'

'I've no idea.'

'Señora, when were you last at Ca'n Mortice?'

'Before we separated.'

'You have not driven there since?'

'Haven't I just said not?'

'Have you ever eaten at Restaurante Monserrat in Runyman?'

'Yes.'

'When?'

'Several times, since it's one of the best in the area and doesn't dumb down the quality of the food for tourists. What's the point of the question?'

'I don't know if there is one.'

'And I believe in fairies dancing on the head of a pin!'

Alvarez drained his glass. 'Thank you for answering all my questions, señora . . .'

Serra called out: 'I'm coming over.'

This time, she did not respond.

He climbed out of the pool and crossed the pool patio, towel in one hand, glass in the other, water draining off his broad-shouldered, slim-waisted, bronzed body. 'So what is the trouble; why are the police here?' he asked, his tone uneasy, his gaze moving from one to the other of them.

She said: 'The inspector's told me a body's been found and it's probably Keith's.'

'Oh! . . . You . . . He . . .' He seemed to swallow further words.

'There must be an identification and I might have to make that. I've said, I don't think I can.' Her voice rose. 'Even the thought of seeing him lying there in God knows what condition makes me feel sick. I can't stand it.'

'Then, my sweet, you mustn't.'

'But what if he tells me I have to?'

'Señora,' Alvarez said, 'as I mentioned, I hope to ask one

119

of the staff to do this and you will only be called on if that proves impracticable.'

'Please, Inspector, try real hard to make certain she doesn't need to,' Serra pleaded. 'You can't really ask her to do such a thing, can you? Not someone like her.'

Annoyed by the other's servile insistence, Alvarez said: 'Is she so very different from any other wife who has to do so?'

'Can't you see that she's too emotional, too responsive to everything? Terrible things overwhelm her.'

He would have judged Serra far more likely to be over-whelmed than she . . . Emotions could be falsely presented. They could also be exposed and exacerbated by guilt . . .

CHAPTER 18

The finca was three kilometres outside Llueso, off the road that led to the centre of the bay. The house, squat, its walls of stone, Roman tiles held down by small rocks and not cement, was much as it had been when built a hundred and fifty years before, the only exceptions being electricity, running water, glass in the windows and a television aerial. The land was not as good as on the plain of Mestara, but nor was it as poor as only a kilometre away. In the fields, divided by walls built generations before from rocks that had been cleared from the soil, there were fig, algarroba, almond, orange, lemon, tangerine, grapefruit, pomegranate and cumquat trees; thanks to the irrigation possible because of a deep, wide, hand-excavated well, melons, tomatoes, peppers, beans, peas, artichokes, lettuces, carrots, radishes, marrows, pumpkins and cucumbers were growing. Immediately in front of the house, over a rusty tubular frame, was an ancient vine with a heavy crop of grapes which would soon start to colour . . . It was the kind of property which Alvarez, in his less unreasonable moments, dreamt of owning, rather than some manorial estate.

Ana, Marti's wife, dressed in shapeless, colourless garments, wide-brimmed straw hat on her head, was using a mattock to redirect a flow of water down an irrigation channel. She looked up briefly as the car came to a stop, then concentrated on her work. Alvarez walked between rows of plants to where she stood, greeted her informally, asked her if her husband was around.

'Gone to the village,' she answered. She opened up the next channel and used the earth she'd excavated to damn the one that had just filled with water.

A man from the towns would have been annoyed by her apparently discourteous indifference to his presence, but Alvarez accepted that in her eyes the needs of the land were far more important than his could ever be. He waited patiently while she worked to the end of that row of channels, then said he'd like a word. She trudged across to the estanque and closed the main outlet by screwing down the gate-valve. She leaned the handle of the mattock against the side of the estanque, built from blocks of sandstone, put her hands in the small of her back and arched her body to relieve the pain. Her face was so lined and leathered, her body so crippled by work, that she could have been almost twice her true age. That was the price paid by her and past generations for working on the land; that was why very few young people were now willing to farm and those who were would not do so in traditional fashion but demanded machinery.

'Why d'you want Gaspar?' she asked, as she brought her hands away from her back. 'Is it because of the señor?'

'That's right.'

'He's gone to the village,' she said again.

'Will he be back soon?'

'Perhaps.'

A true peasant tried never to be specific; there had been times when to be proved wrong might prove fatal. 'Is it all right if I stay on for a while?'

'As you wish.'

'It doesn't look as if you've finished watering?'

'I ain't.'

'Find me a mattock and I'll give a hand.'

'You?'

He nodded.

She hesitated, finally walked over to the house and around to the back; when she returned, she had a second mattock which she handed to him. 'You know what to do?'

'Yes.'

'Don't let the water rise over the channel.'

'I won't.'

122

'Them wants watering,' she said, pointing to several rows of tomato plants which had not been staked, as had become the modern method of growing. She walked to the estanque and opened the main gate-valve.

As he worked, he was amusedly aware that she repeatedly looked in his direction to be certain he was not making a mess of things; she should have been able to judge that when young, he had had to work long hours in the fields to help his parents make enough money for them all to subsist . . . To farm the land, to grow food, was to carry out the most important job any man could do. He was sweating profusely, every movement introduced yet another aching muscle, but he was enjoying the pure pleasure of achievement. From now on, he assured himself, he would regain the true value of life; he'd smoke far less, drink far less, and spend part of every day on the land . . .

She called out that work was finished and went over to the estanque to cut off the water. He mopped his forehead, face and neck with a handkerchief that quickly became sodden. He went across to where she stood.

'Gaspar's not back,' she said, stating the obvious.

He looked at his watch.

'You want to wait some more? Maybe you'd like a drop of wine?'

'Gaspar said you didn't drink.'

'We don't, but that don't stop us offering.'

That seemed to him to be a very rational compromise.

She led the way into the house. But for the paintings, the front room would have lacked any hint of welcome; the floor consisted of rounded pebbles set in Mallorquin cement and had the colour of winter skies, the only furniture was four well-worn chairs with rush seats, an old-fashioned family table with a felt fringe and a charcoal warmer to keep the lower halves of those who sat around it warm whilst the upper halves shivered, and a brass bowl in which a dusty, droopy aspidistra grew. But the five framed paintings all of the same size and attractively framed, vibrated with colour.

'I'll get the wine,' she said and left through the doorway to the right.

Alvarez's fiancée, Juana-María, had been artistic and before her untimely and tragic death many, many years before had introduced him to art in all its forms and tried to persuade him to be as enthusiastic as she; before he'd understood the strength of her appreciation, he had, stupidly, tried to be smart and said that a painting might look pretty, but it was a useless thing since one couldn't plant it or feed it to the animals. It had been several days before she'd forgiven him his ignorant, small-minded comments . . . Each painting depicted a scene from mythology and, thanks to her, he could identify three of the subjects. The knight in full armour approaching a dragon was St George; the man struggling to push a great block of marble up a hill was Sisyphus; the chap with a lyre who had come to a stop and was looking back at the woman who followed was Orpheus . . . Juana-María had asked him, as together they'd looked at an art book, if she were following him out of the Underworld, would he have the self-control not to look back? He'd murmured that if she'd been wearing as little as Eurydice, he'd never have been able to look away even before the start of their journey out of Hades. She giggled so much that her aunt, acting as duenna, had decided it was time they ceased reading together . . .

Ana returned, an earthenware jug in one hand, a glass in the other. She put them on the table. 'Pour for yourself.'

He crossed to the table. The cloudy colour of the wine told him it was home-made and would probably have so harsh and earthy a taste that an oenophile would prefer a glass of acid, but he was going to enjoy every mouthful because he would be reminded of the past when his parents had been alive. He filled the glass, sat, drank. 'It's real good,' he said.

She looked pleased.

The sense of well-being compelled him to compliment her on the paintings. 'They look nice on the walls,' he said, with a broad wave of his free hand. 'They were clever blokes who painted those!'

'It was Gaspar,' she said.

For the moment, he thought she'd not understood what he'd said. 'I mean the blokes who actually painted them.'

'It were Gaspar.'

Because all five had been executed with such skill and assurance, he'd assumed that they were reproductions and only now did he understand that they possessed such vibrancy because they were not. 'You mean, he painted them?'

'Isn't that what I'm saying?'

He swore at himself for showing such obvious surprise. He should have known that apparent character could be a poor indication of the true person; behind Marti's dour exterior, there lurked a man who not only understood beauty and emotion, but could try to express them in paint.

'Been doing it since he was a kid. There was a priest what told him to get taught because he'd be real good, but there wasn't no money for anything like that . . . He copied 'em from a book of paintings I bought with some money I'd saved. He said he was angry I'd spent it on that, but really he was pleased . . . Of course, the elders don't like him doing such things.'

'The elders?' he queried.

She didn't try to explain. 'They say that sort of thing shows the sin of pride and to paint women is the sin of desire. But there wasn't nothing like that – he did 'em for me. Still, because they'd spoke, he didn't do no more for a while. Then they came here again the other day and saw as he'd done that one after they'd said to stop and they were so angry they told him to burn 'em all.'

He looked at the painting she'd indicated. A woman, her body hardly concealed by the diaphanous clothes she wore, a necklace of flowers about her throat, was riding an animal towards the sea, in which was a male figure armed with a trident and around whom a dolphin played; many nymphs, even more scantily clad than she, followed. To a healthy man, a very attractive scene; to a prude, a prig, the devil in many forms . . .

'He was against burning 'em because they were mine. And I told 'em, I wasn't going to. So they said we had to leave the brotherhood.' She stared into space. 'I just wouldn't,' she said, with sudden force, all the more marked because until then she had been speaking quietly.

'If the paintings were mine,' he said, 'I wouldn't burn 'em if a couple of archangels came down and told me to.'

Gratified by his words, she stared at each painting in turn, seeing something that no one else would ever discern.

They heard a car come to a stop and a moment later, Marti entered the house. He stared at Alvarez. 'It's still thirsty weather, then?'

'The sun's shining.'

'With the likes of you, it'll be shining at midnight. What do you want?'

'To ask you a couple of questions.'

'What?'

'A body's been washed ashore on Cap Parelona and it's likely Señor Vickers's. Will you identify it?'

'Why me?'

'Señora Vickers is naturally very reluctant to have to do this and so I'd like to find someone else. Will you do it?'

Marti shrugged his shoulders.

'If you come to the post at ten tomorrow morning . . .' He stopped. Ten would interfere with his merienda. 'Make that half past ten. We'll drive into Palma and you can identify him.'

Marti again said nothing.

'There's something I need to know. In the past three to four weeks, have you seen Señora Vickers near Ca'n Mortice?'

'No.'

'Not anywhere along the track to the road?'

'No.'

'How about a twenty-year-old man, well-built, around a metre eighty-two to eighty-five, tall, curly black hair, dark-brown eyes, a round face and a bit of a woman's mouth?'

'All I've seen were the three putas.'

'Why d'you call them that?'

'They were sunbathing naked. And when they saw me they just laughed.'

126

Alvarez wondered why life so often offered pleasure to someone unwilling to enjoy it. 'That's about everything, then. I'll be on my way.'

'Are you leaving before the bottle's empty?'

'Are you suggesting I refill my glass?'

'No.'

'I'm leaving.'

CHAPTER 19

As Alvarez entered the room, the phone rang. The secretary with a plum-filled voice said that the superior chief wished to speak to him and as he waited, he congratulated himself on not arriving at the office more than half an hour late.

'I've received no report from you on the Vickers case,' was Salas's greeting.

'Señor, that is because –'

'You have done nothing, perhaps?'

'Because I am pursuing many leads and, knowing you always wish a report to be complete, I have been trying to make certain which ones are relevant and which are not before advising you. I have spoken to Señora Vickers and shown her the signet ring from the dead man's finger – she says it is the one she gave her husband as an engagement present.'

'You are saying you have positively identified the body?'

'No, señor. As you will have immediately foreseen, one has to remember that there is the possibility of the ring having been switched. That is why I have arranged to drive Marti, the gardener, to Palma to view the body.'

'Why is the putative widow not doing that?'

'Señora Vickers expressed a strong reluctance to do so . . .'

'Since when have you consulted a witness's wishes rather than followed the rules of procedure?'

'There seemed no point in subjecting her to so emotional a task.'

'Refrain from judgements that are not yours to make.'

'But Marti is as capable of identifying the body as Señora Vickers; one could say, even more qualified, since he has been

129

seeing the señor every day whilst the señora has only done so once in many months.'

'You are suggesting a person's appearance will change radically in just months?'

'I was explaining –'

'Usually I find slightly less difficulty in understanding you when you do not explain what you are saying.'

'In the circumstances, and since Marti has agreed to go with me to the morgue at the Institute of Forensic Anatomy, would it not be best to continue with the arrangement?'

There was no answer.

'Having spoken to Señora Vickers, it became obvious Serra is her lover . . .'

'I wondered how long it would be before you could find reason for introducing at least one salacious detail.'

'But I am certain that fact could be pertinent . . .'

'Who are Vickers's beneficiaries?'

'The señora could not tell me.'

'Was he about to change his will?'

'She knows very little about his financial affairs.'

'Have you determined who is his abogado?'

'By the time I returned from speaking with Marti –'

'An efficient member of the Cuerpo would, by now, have searched through all the papers at Ca'n Mortice to discover the answers to those questions. You will go there now and . . .'

'Señor, as I said earlier, I am driving Marti into Palma a little later on. It seemed to me important to confirm the dead man is Señor Vickers before trying to find out about his financial affairs.'

'Then why are you not already in Palma?'

'Marti was unable to get away before ten-thirty.'

'If the rest of the world lived at the same pace as you Mallorquins, humanity would still be in the Stone Age.' Salas cut the connection.

Alvarez checked the time to see how long it would be before he needed to go to Club Llueso for his morning coffee and a small brandy.

*   *   *

Marti was not a mentally stimulating travelling companion. Alvarez tried to discuss the benefits of growing tomatoes upright on canes as opposed to letting them bush out unsupported; on planting Scottish seed potatoes rather than Spanish ones; on which variety of French beans grew best in the heat of the summer; on the advent of yellow peppers in the shops, but not yet in the ground; on whether avocado pears were financially profitable . . . If Marti had an opinion, it was delivered abruptly and with sufficient aggression to make it obvious he would not listen to any argument; if he had no firm opinion, he remained silent.

They parked in the forecourt of the Institute, went down to the basement. An assistant led the way into a room, one side of which was lined with refrigerated compartments, checked a list, slid out the holding trolley of No. 14. He pulled back the sheet to reveal the corpse's face.

Death had been tidied up, but even so, Alvarez mentally shivered. One day perhaps it would be he who was slid out of the cold so that he could be identified . . .

'It's him,' Marti said.

'You are quite certain that is the body of Señor Vickers?'

'You think I'm blind?'

'Right. Then you go back to the car and I'll be along in a minute.'

Marti left.

'A cheerful soul!' the assistant said, as he returned the body.

'He belongs to a sect which seems to think it's a sin to do anything except suffer.'

'Then I say, suffer hard and long and enjoy it. I'd an aunt who owned three fincas and got tied up with some weirdies. Left 'em everything. The family tried to get a fair share, but ended up with almost nothing. If the properties were ours now, they'd be worth a couple of hundred million . . . Like they say, if you've a rich relative, you'll find reason to hate all the people she likes.'

'True enough . . . Is Professor Fortunato in the building?'

131

'Someone said he was off to a conference in Italy today.'

Alvarez thanked the other, made his way up to the professor's office where his secretary suggested he spoke to Garcia.

Garcia, small of stature, short of hair on his head but with a luxuriant full beard, shook hands, suggested he sat, searched through the files on the desk and found the one he wanted. He brought out from this several pages, skimmed through these, looked up. 'The official report will be with you as soon as we can draw it up, but you can take it that it won't be any different from what I can tell you now. The blow to the back of the head fractured the skull and rendered Vickers unconscious. He was then thrown into the water and actual death was due to drowning; evidence confirms this occurred in salt water. Marks on the right ankle cannot be positively identified, but our judgement is that rope or cord was tied around it, with a weight attached, and this subsequently pulled free – probably a duff knot, gradually untied by the slight motion of the sea. The deep wound to the stomach was inflicted with a horn.'

'What?'

'I know! Kind of makes you wonder what sort of a world we live in . . . Initially, all we could say was something that was reasonably pointed and had an increasing diameter had been thrust deeply into his body causing considerable internal injury. Then from within the body we recovered a sliver of what has been identified as horn – probably from a bull or cow, but typically the lab boys won't yet express any certainty. Such a horn would account for the injuries sustained.'

'When was this – before or after the blow to the head?'

'Can't be certain, but probably after.'

Confirmation of what the doctor had surmised after the body had been found – plus some additional, perplexing evidence . . .

'The blow to the head was delivered with a metallic bar some two to two and a half centimetres in diameter when the victim was turned away from the striker. We have found flecks of a light-green paint with red lead under-neath.'

Alvarez recalled that the yacht's upperworks were painted a light-green. The murderer had picked up a stanchion, or something of that nature, wielded it with brutal force, and probably used it as a weight . . .

He thanked the other, left and returned to his car.

'Time obviously don't mean anything to the likes of you,' Marti observed sourly. 'I've sat here long enough to take root.'

'I needed to talk to one of the pathologists.' He started the engine, backed the car in a wide semi-circle. 'It's been your job to clean the yacht, hasn't it?'

'The outside. It's women's work to clean the inside.'

'D'you know much about the *Valhalla*?'

'Nothing except it takes a long time to wash it down.'

The answer had been so forcefully spoken that Alvarez smiled. 'Boats aren't your idea of fun?'

'A bloody stupid way of wasting money.'

He drove out on to the road. Once in the middle stream of traffic, he said: 'Where would you look to find a bull's or cow's horn?'

'On a bull or cow.'

Ask a sensible question and get a stupid answer.

CHAPTER 20

Back in his office, Alvarez phoned Melanie Lockwood. 'Señorita, I am afraid I have some sad news.'

Her response was immediate. 'Keith's dead?'

'His body has been discovered washed up in a cove on Cap Parelona.'

'Oh!' There was a long pause. 'I was still hoping that . . . He said once that he wasn't a good swimmer. I told him he must wear a life jacket all the time he was at sea. He just laughed at the idea. He was a seaman and couldn't fall over the side . . . I always thought . . .'

'You thought what, señorita?'

'That the real reason was, it would have ruined the image. Wouldn't suit the yachting cap worn at a salty angle. He saw himself as . . . Christ! Why am I talking like this? What's it matter now how he saw himself?'

He thought it likely she was suffering from the nervous uneasiness many experienced when death was announced rather than shock which came from savaged emotions. Or perhaps she was seeing a dream fade. 'It was not an accident.'

'How d'you mean?'

'Señor Vickers was murdered.'

'Oh, my God! It's a nightmare.'

'Because of this, I need to talk to you. Perhaps you can help me identify who might be guilty.'

'But . . . but I can't tell you anything.'

'Señorita, I understand you may not have any direct knowledge of importance, but it is possible that even though you don't realize this, you do know something that must interest me. When would it be convenient for me to come and see you?'

After a while, she said: 'When do you want to?'

'This afternoon, at five-thirty?'

She hesitantly replied that that would be all right. He asked her where she lived and made a note of her answer. Then, having said goodbye, he phoned Rosa and asked her: 'Is there a safe in the house?'

'A large one, behind what looks like just a door.'

'Does it have a combination lock?'

'What's that?'

He described what this would look like and her answer made it clear that the safe had one such. 'Do you know what the correct combination is?'

A simple question that created a complicated problem. She thought he was implying she might frequently open the safe to help herself to the odd ten-thousand-peseta note; it took him time to persuade her that the only reason for the question was the fact that some safe owners stupidly left a note of the combination lying around. He finally convinced her that her honesty had not been impugned. 'Will you go now and have a look at the safe and see if there's a maker's name and reference number?'

She returned to the phone to tell him there was a small brass plate on which were both a name and a number. He wrote these down, thanked her, said he'd probably be along the next morning.

There was just time to make one more phone call before he left to return home. He spoke to the manager of the firm in Palma which did any necessary lock work for the Cuerpo.

'You say you want someone for tomorrow?'

'That's right.'

'But it's Saturday.'

He wondered how he could have overlooked that fact? But with Salas breathing down his neck . . . 'All days are the same for us when there's work to be done. So if he's here by ten . . .'

'It's an hour's drive. Make it eleven.'

The sooner the job was completed, the sooner the week-end could begin. Even merienda could be hurried. 'Sorry, but

136

with the pressure we're under, every minute has to be made to do an hour's work.'

'You must be as exhausted as hell by the end of a day, then!'

True.

San Martin Vell was fifteen kilometres inland and in consequence had escaped most of the disasters of tourism while enjoying many of the benefits; the surrounding land was in good heart and there was virtually limitless water for irrigation so that three crops in a year could be grown.

The streets were narrow, often too narrow for cars to pass each other, and frequently they ended in different directions from those in which they had started. There was a saying on the island, 'As twisted as the roads of San Martin'. It cost Alvarez time and temper to find the house near the corner of the crossroads.

He stepped through the opened doorway protected by a fly curtain made from strips of plastic, into a front room furnished for appearance rather than comfort, immaculately clean and called out. An old woman shuffled through the inner doorway, came to a halt and stared stolidly at a space to his right. 'I'm looking for Señorita Lockwood,' he said.

There was no response.

'She said she lives here.'

She chewed her upper lip between near-toothless gums. 'Who are you?'

'Cuerpo General de Policia.'

She finally showed some interest. 'She's been up to something?'

'Up to nothing. So where can I find her?'

'Upstairs.'

'How do I get there?'

'Up the stairs.'

He couldn't decide whether she was simple-minded or enjoying trying to make him look a fool. 'Suppose you show me where these are?'

A narrow passage ran the length of the house and gave

access to a very small, enclosed garden in which a couple of sad-looking tangerine trees grew; a flight of wooden steps led up to the top floor. The outer door of the flat was open, but since a foreigner lived there, he knocked and waited. Melanie appeared. Dressed in a T-shirt that was tighter than a maiden aunt would have suggested, and shorts that were shorter, she possessed the kind of figure that made a man's hands tingle . . . He introduced himself.

'Come on in.'

She moved with an evocative grace . . . He pulled his thoughts together. Nothing was more useless than a daydream unless one possessed either youth or fortune. She asked him if he'd like a drink and he tried not to watch her as she went across to a table on which were several bottles and glasses, but when she bent over, the T-shirt tightened even further . . .

It needed little prompting on his part to learn that she worked as a courier and lived in San Martin Vell because rents were so much cheaper than nearer the coast; also, when off duty, she was unlikely to be called if there were an emergency. She'd worked for the same firm for three years and hoped soon to be made area manager . . .

'Señorita, when and where did you meet Señor Vickers?'

She looked at him, then away and down at her glass. 'How was he . . . ?'

'A blow to the head knocked him unconscious and he fell, or was pushed, into the sea and drowned.'

She drank. 'Who could do such a terrible thing?'

'I'm here to try and find out.'

She drained her glass. 'I need another. Would you like one?' She stood.

He handed her his glass.

'It's not that I didn't know . . .' She took the glass from him, crossed to the table. 'Have you ever hated yourself?'

Her question so surprised him that it was several seconds before he said: 'Frequently. It has to be a stupidly self-satisfied person who doesn't.'

'When he didn't arrive to pick me up at the port, where I

was waiting, I started wondering if he'd met someone else and decided to stand me up. Then I saw myself becoming jealous over a man twice my age and not exactly a heart throb and realized that because of the yacht, the expensive restaurants, the promise of a luxury cruise, I was . . . When he talked about marriage, I was certain he did that to every girlfriend yet I still wanted to believe him. I was born in suburbia and he seemed to be offering Park Lane. I lied to myself again and again . . .'

He listened to what was more an attempt to understand her own confused emotions than a confession. Many would have condemned her attitude, but he did not. As the old Mallorquin saw put it, Love follows money as eagerly as the ram follows the ewe.

She filled the glasses and handed him one, unaware of how long she had been standing by the table. She settled on her chair.

He asked her a second time: 'When and where did you meet Señor Vickers?'

She spoke both quickly and slowly, reliving moments she could recall with pleasure and moments she could not. Several weeks previously, she'd been told by the concierge at one of the hotels that a newly arrived tourist was complaining loudly and bitterly about the cold rain and strong wind when the firm's brochure had promised endless hot sunshine. Mentally composing a politely sarcastic explanation that the weather was beyond her or her firm's control, she'd approached Vickers, believing him to be the complainant. Never one to miss an opportunity, within five minutes of discovering her mistake, he'd suggested dinner at the Estrella, and she'd accepted even though normally she steered clear of older men because they were either boringly or insultingly eager. Estrella was a chic restaurant, recently opened in the foothills of the Sierra de Torrellas. Normally, she'd never have eaten there, but it was only the first of many expensive restaurants to which he'd taken her. He'd tried to seduce her at Ca'n Mortice and on *Valhalla*. Each attempt had been accompanied by protestations of love and the prospect of a

139

life of luxurious bliss. Her stubborn defence had increased his lust but, strangely, not aroused his annoyance. At one point she'd wondered if her resistance was affording him added pleasure because his triumph would be that much greater when attained, as he'd no doubt it would be. For her part, she'd promised herself that her submission was very far from certain, knowing that she was lying. 'I really liked him.'

The truth? A lie to ease her conscience because she couldn't escape the certainty that her sense of loss was not emotional? 'During the time you knew the señor, did he ever say or do anything to suggest he thought he might be in danger?'

'I don't think so. I suppose there was the time he said there were several people in the world who wished him six feet under, but it seemed to me he was really jeering at them because they couldn't do anything to harm him.'

'He didn't name anyone or explain why they might wish him dead?'

'It was something to do with business; that's all I know.'

'When did you last see him?'

'Two days before . . . before he died. We went to the casino and he gave me a hundred thousand to play with. I won thirty thousand. And as we left, he said we obviously had . . .'

'Had what?'

'A . . . a lucky future.' She swallowed heavily. 'Some bloody luck!'

'But all that evening, he seemed perfectly happy and at ease?'

'Yes.'

'Señorita, there is a question I have to ask even though I am sure you will find it an objectionable one . . .'

'He never made first base.'

It took him a moment to understand what she meant. 'That is not what I was going to ask.'

She picked up her glass and drained it.

'Do you know if he was friendly with someone else when he first met you?'

'There had been someone.'

'Can you tell me anything about her?'

'Only that her name was Serena.'

'Can you say where she went after they parted?'

'I've no idea.'

That answer might or might not be true, but there seemed no point in pursuing the matter for the moment. He thanked her for her help, and left.

CHAPTER 21

Flusa, the locksmith, was a tall, thin, sombre, disgruntled Catalan. When Alvarez suggested he followed in his own car to Ca'n Mortice, he asked how far this would be, then said he'd leave his in the village and travel in Alvarez's. Catalans devoted their lives to saving a peseta.

Halfway up the twisting climb out of Port Llueso, Alvarez stopped the Ibiza, pointed at the bay spread out below them, and enthusiastically suggested that there was nothing more beautiful this side of Arcadia. Flusa bluntly observed that in a short drive southwards from La Mortera, where he had been born, one could see at least two bays that were more attractive.

The cove at Ca'n Mortice was at its most vibrant, with the sun at an angle that dimpled the pellucid water with sparkles. Alvarez refrained from any enthusiastic comment, certain that if he made one he'd be assured that along the Costa Brava there were a dozen coves to overawe this one . . .

As he studied the large safe, Flusa said: 'It's going to take time.'

'How long?'

'How can I give an estimate before I even begin?'

By trying, perhaps?

'Presumably you've made certain that a note of the combination hasn't been hidden somewhere, for instance under that desk?'

'I haven't found one,' Alvarez answered correctly.

Flusa opened the small suitcase he'd carried with him and from this brought out three different-sized electronic instruments, two of which he placed on the closed lid of the case; he connected the third and largest to the safe with a magnetic clasp, began slowly to revolve the outer dial of the combination lock as he studied the readings on the illuminated scale.

Alvarez wandered over to the window and stared out at the cove as he tried to work out his best move for the immediate future. If the safe were opened quickly, he could drive Flusa back to Llueso and be home for lunch; if it took as long as Flusa's pessimistic attitude suggested, he could leave the other at work, have lunch at home, and return in the afternoon after a brief siesta; but if success lay between those two limits, he might be at home, about to start eating, when Flusa rang and demanded to be collected then and there . . .

He went through to the kitchen. Luisa was there, as well as Rosa, and in a temper because Rosa had told her she had to turn up even if it was a Saturday and even if she thought she might be developing double pneumonia; they were cleaning the contents of a canteen of Queen's pattern silver cutlery. Rosa looked down at the fork in her left hand. 'It's odd, isn't it?'

'What is?' he asked.

'Us doing this because the señor demands the silver is kept polished. But he ain't here any more and so maybe none of this will be used until it all becomes tarnished and so we're just wasting our time.'

'Most of what we do is a waste of time,' Luisa observed.

'Only if you do it badly.'

'It's nothing to do with that. I dust the sitting room today – really dust it, and you won't find anything swept under the carpet, whatever you think – and tomorrow it all needs doing again. So what have you gained, that's what I want to know?'

'You've got to be the modern generation to think like that.'

'Or sensible.'

Rosa sniffed loudly. She turned to Alvarez. 'Have you come in to say you'd like some coffee?'

'That's one of the things I was going to mention.'

'I'll make it,' Luisa said quickly.

'It's nice to see you so eager to do something!'

'This job makes my fingernails filthy and I just can't get 'em clean for days. Ricardo hates dirty fingernails.'

'I'm surprised if that's what he spends his time bothering about.'

'Men aren't all like you think they are.'

'You've a lot to learn.'

Luisa washed her hands in the sink, complained the muck wouldn't shift from under her nails, began to prepare the coffee machine. Rosa said, as she polished: 'So the other man is opening the safe?'

'Hopefully he is,' Alvarez answered. 'Have you ever seen inside it?'

'When I've gone into the library and he's had it open.'

'Is there much in it?'

'Lots of papers. And then there's several small boxes what likely have jewellery in them.'

'Is there a lot of that?'

'Can't rightly say. I've seen a fair amount because he gives his women bits to wear, but I wouldn't know how much there is I ain't seen.'

'I've been told he was friendly with Serena before he met Señorita Lockwood – is that right?'

'She was one before. The last was Emma.'

'No, she wasn't,' Luisa said. 'She was the last woman to live here and Emma was the one before.'

'It was Emma last.'

'I'll tell you how I can prove you wrong.'

'Oh, you can, can you?' Rosa's tone was sarcastic.

'You remember Emma coming back?'

'So?'

'It was last autumn, wasn't it?'

'What if it was?'

'Serena was here at Christmas – you came and said, "She's been telling me what sort of a party she'll have next Christmas because she thinks the señor's going to marry her and she'll be the señora and if that happens, I'll be off because she'll be a real bitch."'

145

'I didn't use such a word.'

'And you added another!'

Alvarez decided that Rosa's silence meant not only that she had described Serena in very uncomplimentary terms, but that she now realized her mistake and Serena had been the previous girlfriend as Melanie had told him. 'Do either of you know what's happened to Serena?'

'She's in Italy,' Rosa answered.

'How do you know that?'

'The señor told me she was and if ever she was to phone him again, we was to say he was away on a cruise . . . There's none of 'em with the sense to see the kind of man he really is. I mean, was.'

'That's true enough!' Luisa said. 'You'll remember Emma?'

Rosa carefully did not answer.

'Came back to see him and when I said he wasn't here – which was the truth – she wrote down her new address and telephone number because she was so certain he'd want her back, but wouldn't know how to find her.'

'Did you give the señor that information?' he asked.

'Rosa said not to bother, he wouldn't be interested.'

'It would only have put him in a temper,' Rosa snapped.

'So what did you do with the note she gave you?'

'I put it in the drawer where we keep that sort of thing in case.'

'In case of what?'

'We might need it – whatever she thinks.' Luisa looked briefly at Rosa.

'Is there any chance it'll still be there?'

'Maybe.'

'Will you have a look for it, then?'

'I suppose I could.' Luisa went over to one of the built-in units, pulled open the top drawer.

The coffee maker hissed. Rosa switched off the gas, washed her hands, set three mugs, a bowl of sugar, and a carton of milk on the table. 'You'll probably like a coñac with the coffee?'

He agreed he probably would.

She poured coffee into the three mugs, brought a half-full bottle of Soberano out of a cupboard.

Luisa said: 'There you are!' She handed Alvarez a crumpled square of paper.

Emma Oakley, 15, Carrer General Jodar, Montagut. Very occasionally, there was a time when luck ran with, instead of against, one.

Thirty-five minutes later, he returned to the library. Flusa might not have moved other than slowly to revolve the dials. 'How's it going?' he asked. 'Will it take much longer?'

'It will take as long as it takes.'

Good logic, but typical Catalan rudeness. Alvarez checked the time yet again and finally accepted that he would not be returning home for lunch . . . His mood lightened. Surely Rosa must be a good cook or Vickers would not have employed her? He returned to the kitchen. Rosa said she'd be happy to provide a meal.

He rang home to tell Dolores that due to work he would not be returning for lunch . . .

'On a Saturday?' she said sharply.

'I had to drive both of us here . . .'

'Your companion no doubt is a young woman?'

'A middle-aged locksmith who's trying to open a safe.' He could picture her expression of disbelief. 'Shall I ask him to come to the phone and tell you who he is and what he's doing?'

'When a man knows you can't see his face, he lies twice as hard.'

He said a dignified goodbye and rang off. Back in the kitchen, Rosa said: 'I thought we could have chuletas de cordero con pimientos asados.'

'This is my lucky day! That's my favourite dish,' he assured her, knowing how encouragement could fire a cook to even greater skills.

Rosa prepared to grill several peppers. 'Luisa, suppose you rub the cutlets with paprika, salt and plenty of black pepper?'

'I'm off home.'

147

'There's another half-hour to go for your time.'

Luisa silently swore.

'The meal will be a while,' Rosa said, 'so help yourself to another drink when you want one.'

He refilled his glass, added ice. 'Gaspar told me he never cleans inside the yacht, but one of you two do that.'

'He's too bloody stubborn to do any more than he thinks he has to,' Luisa said.

'That's enough of that sort of language!' Rosa snapped. 'And cleaning ain't a man's job.'

'Ricardo says he's not going to leave me to do everything about the house when we're married.'

'Remind him of that when you are.'

Alvarez hastened to divert the conversation. 'Have either of you ever seen an animal's horn when you've been cleaning the inside of the boat?'

'There wasn't nothing like that,' Rosa said.

'Yes, there was,' Luisa contradicted.

'No, there wasn't.'

'What about the thing in the saloon, then?'

'What thing?'

Luisa didn't immediately answer and her manner began to suggest she regretted having spoken.

'Well?' There was a note of triumph in Rosa's voice. 'You need to learn you'd best keep quiet when you've nothing sensible to say.'

'It was . . .' She began, became silent.

Alvarez prompted her. 'There was something on the boat that looked like a horn?'

Luisa fiddled with a button on her dress.

'Tell me about it.'

'I didn't mean to knock it over.'

'You broke something?' Rosa quickly said.

'Someone left it in a stupid place and since that wasn't me, it was likely you.'

He hastened to prevent an angry argument. 'Tell me what happened.'

One day, Luisa had accidentally knocked the object over

148

and a piece of horn, near the tip, had broken off. She'd been chewing gum, so she'd used some to stick the piece back on and unless one had looked closely, it had been impossible to tell . . .

'If the señor had ever discovered what you'd done, he'd have sacked you,' Rosa said with satisfaction.

'Well, he didn't. And he's not going to get the chance now, is he?'

'I've always told you, you don't look what you're doing.'

'If someone leaves something in a stupid place it doesn't matter how hard I look.'

Alvarez once more hastily intervened. 'What exactly did this object look like?'

Luisa had difficulty in giving a good description and Rosa – her memory jolted – provided a clearer picture. On a square, black wooden stand, a polished horn had been mounted on a slender silver column that supported it at the point of balance so that when seen sideways-on, the horn was a graceful curve. This had not been on the yacht when he'd made his search. 'Do you know anything about it?'

'I once asked the señor, when he seemed in a good mood, where it came from,' Luisa said. 'He told me it was from the toro bravo at the bull running at Pamplona the year he took part. Know what I think? The likes of him wouldn't go anywhere near the bulls at the running – they just watch from one of the balconies. He bought the horn somewhere to try to persuade his women what a brave man he was.'

'You shouldn't keep talking about him like you do now he's dead,' Rosa protested.

'Being dead don't make him brave.'

Alvarez absent-mindedly refilled his glass and added ice. Vickers might have bought the object because its shape attracted him, or there might be truth in what Luisa suggested; in either case, the question of where the horn had come from was almost certainly established.

Flusa had eaten quickly, careless of the quality of the cooking, and had drunk only half a glassful of the Marqués de Cáceres;

Alvarez had eaten like a good trencherman and drunk three glassfuls of the excellent wine. While Rosa washed up – Luisa had left before the meal – he'd decided to walk down to the pool and relax for a moment . . .

He awoke to find Rosa standing by his side.

'He says to tell you he's opened the safe.'

It took him a moment to pull his mind together and understand what she was talking about. When he did, he thanked her, followed her back up the slope, albeit it at a slower pace.

Flusa lacked any sense of modesty. He pointed to the open safe and remarked that although of an old pattern, the lock mechanism was of the finest quality and he doubted there was another man on the island, even perhaps south of Madrid, who could have succeeded in doing what he had. 'You can drive me back to my car now.'

'I'll need to make a preliminary check of the contents first.'

'As quickly as you can, then. It is Saturday afternoon.'

He hardly needed reminding of that fact.

There were five jewel boxes of different sizes, which contained pieces of jewellery which to his uneducated eyes looked valuable. There were three hundred and forty thousand pesetas, in ten-thousand-peseta notes; cheque books on five different banks in three countries; numerous bank statements; two account books, one covering current expenditure, the other capital; files of paper; and several folders, one of which was marked 'Will'. Inside this were two wills and two letters. Under the Spanish will, all assets in Spain were left to the trustees named in the Jersey will; under the latter, all assets were to be given to the Vickers Foundation which would engage in general charitable work, subject only to sufficient capital being retained by the trustees, who would invest it at their discretion, to pay his wife, Laura Nancy Vickers, the agreed allowance for her lifetime. Both letters were from the same firm of solicitors in London. The first stated that counsel's opinion had been received and this was to the effect that the agreement under which his wife received an allowance had been drawn up inexpertly and there should be little trouble in having it declared void. The second stated that steps to have the agreement held void would be taken on receipt of instructions, but Vickers should understand there had to be the possibility his wife would challenge the action in the British courts. However, in view of the difficulties inevitably experienced when parties lived, and their assets were held, overseas, there could be no certainty that even if successful in court, she would ever be able to have the terms of a judgement enforced . . .

He was certain that now he knew why Laura Vickers had met her husband on that single occasion after their separation.

CHAPTER 22

Alvarez altered the angle of the fan on the desk to try to gain more benefit from its draught, sat back in the chair. Bank statements, cheque books and account books, could be sent to an accountant to judge whether there was anything of significance to be found amongst the mass of figures, but it was proving very difficult to work out how to avoid having to read through all the correspondence, contents of files . . .

The phone rang. The superior chief wished to speak to him.

'I have just had the Director General on the line. He asked me, were all my inspectors incompetent? I tried to assure him that only one was and that I could hardly be held accountable for his appointment since that took place before I became commander of the Cuerpo on the island.'

'Has something happened, señor?'

'Only you could ask that after having repeatedly insulted an important member of the British government and then compounded that dire stupidity by demanding his passport on the grounds that he was a murderer.'

'All I asked Señor Lovell to do was to answer my question. And you agreed that when it became certain Señor Vickers had been murdered and had not died in an accident, Señor Lovell must explain the nature of the row on the Thursday morning because –'

'I agreed to no such thing.'

'When I spoke to you –'

'I made it clear that my concern was to try to repair the damage you had caused . . . Unfortunately, that was an impossibility. It has been made known to the Director

153

General that there are those in England who are surprised that, despite previous representation, we have seen fit to continue to persecute Señor Lovell.'

'There's never been any persecution. And surely now that this is a murder case, no foreign authority has the right to interfere in the case?'

'Interfere? Who has mentioned anything about interfering?'

'You've just said the Director General has received a complaint . . .'

'I said no such thing. Good God, man, are you so naive you can imagine that in a matter like this, a direct complaint is made? Such an action would be against all convention and however much one must condemn the British for their perfidiousness, their immorality, and their drunken tourists, they usually observe diplomatic niceties. A remark was casually passed during a reception at which members of both British and Spanish governments were present.'

'Then it's not official and we don't have to take any notice of it . . .'

'There are times when I wonder if you inhabit the same world as the rest of humanity. Tell me, in your confusion, have you done anything further to persecute Señor Lovell so that I need to warn the Director General that the worst is yet to come?'

'I have spent the day at Ca'n Mortice, helping the locksmith break open the safe there. Inside were the señor's two wills, one Spanish, one English, and two letters from solicitors in England. It is clear that he intended to break his agreement to pay his wife a generous allowance. Had he lived, the probability is that Señora Vickers would have been left very badly off. This raises a clear motive . . .'

'And makes your suspicions concerning Señor Lovell all the more ridiculous. You will apologize to him for your stupidity; when you do so, you will make it absolutely clear that from the beginning of this sad and sorry affair, you have been acting totally on your own account; you will admit you have even failed to inform your superiors of your actions, certain they would unreservedly have condemned them had you done so. Is that clear?'

'Does that mean I am to return Señor Lovell's passport even if he continues to refuse to explain the row between Señor Vickers and himself?'

'Since you saw fit to confiscate it, the decision will be yours.' Salas cut the connection.

Damned if he did, damned if he didn't.

Geraldine opened the front door of Ca Na Atalla. 'Good morning, Inspector. Do come in.'

As Alvarez stepped into the hall, Dale came through the doorway to the left. 'Are you by any chance here for another word with George?'

'I should like to speak with Señor Lovell, yes, if that is convenient?'

'Convenient to whom? ... A whisper in your ear. In today's copy of *The Times*, there is an article naming those members of the government who it is held are doing a good job; through some unfortunate oversight of the author of the article, George's name has been omitted and this is causing much distress. As Congreve did not write, Nor Hell a fury, like a politician forgotten. So be prepared for a degree of aggrieved annoyance.'

'For downright bad temper,' she said. 'Inspector, is there any chance he will be allowed to leave soon?'

'I am here to return his passport, señora.'

'Esme, ring the travel agent and book the first available flight – business, economy class, whatever; the baggage hold if necessary.'

'If there's any problem, I'll leave it to George to have them send out Concorde. Our present government couldn't possibly resist the temptation to spend a small fortune on one of themselves ... Carry on through to the pool, Inspector, and may the force be with you.'

Lovell, in swimming trunks, was sitting in the shade of a sun umbrella set through the middle of a patio table on the far side of the pool. He watched Alvarez approach, said nothing.

'Good morning, señor.'

'What do you want?'

'To hand you back your passport.'

'Where is it?'

Alvarez brought it out of his pocket and passed it across.

'Someone has finally seen fit to use some common sense!'

'The decision as to what to do was left in my hands.'

'Clearly, I was mistaken.'

'Señor, now that you have your passport, would you be kind enough to explain what the row was about that you had with Señor Vickers?'

'Have I not made it perfectly clear a dozen and one times that I am incapable of explaining something that did not happen?'

'It would help the investigation . . .'

'I suggest a change of investigator might be of far greater assistance.'

Alvarez said goodbye.

Dale was in the sitting room. 'That was short and sharp rather than sweet, presumably?'

'As sour as an unripe persimmon, señor.'

'Then you need something to sweeten life. Am I correct in remembering you like brandy with just ice?'

Alvarez watched a gecko cross the ceiling with its ridiculous waggling, scrambling movement. What was life as a gecko like? There would be no having to deal with the endless problems of others, no autocratic English politicians, no superior chief to turn life into an obstacle race; on the other hand, a very restricted diet. Would that fact ever occur to a gecko? If one had never eaten lechóna with special crackling that sparkled every taste bud in the mouth, could one regret the absence of it?

He phoned Vadell. 'I need to question someone who lives in your patch so shall I call in at your post and we'll go on together?'

'Is that necessary? Is the case going to cause me bother?'

'Most unlikely.'

156

'Then go ahead on your own.'

'Don't forget that memorandum from Salas about procedure when an inspector needs to work in another's area . . .'

'I've forgotten it.'

'So it's all right with you if I handle matters on my own?'

'Why make both of us busy? . . . Have you heard the latest about Salas? When he was in Salamanca . . .'

The story was so amusingly obscene that Alvarez tried hard to believe it.

Montagut, once a fishing village, lay on the east side of an inlet which ran for several hundred metres in a north-westerly direction between rocky walls; had the inlet been considerably wider, this would probably have been one of the major boating centres on the island because the water was deep and there was protection from most winds, but as it was, the number of moorings was of necessity very limited. The old village was almost unchanged, with narrow, twisting roads; the new, which ringed the old, was set on higher ground and consisted of a mixture of bungalows, houses, and apartment blocks. Because the beaches were pebbled and there were few bars and no discothèques, it was not a resort that was popular with families with children or youngsters in search of life – its greatest attraction to those who chose to holiday there.

Carrer General Jodar was a curving, narrow, gradually ascending road; the terrace houses directly fronted the road and unless great care was taken when stepping out of one of them, this could be a life-threatening experience, thanks to the local drivers. Most houses had been reformed and many now had rock walls exposed; a few had not and their battered exteriors incorrectly suggested hardship or even poverty – it was taking time for elderly owners to accept that money spent on property was well spent.

Number 15, unreformed, was halfway up the road and when Alvarez stepped into the front room and called out, an elderly woman, wearing widow's grey, came through the inner doorway. He asked her where Emma Oakley lived. In the fewest possible words – it was said that the people of

Montagut were so parsimonious their alphabet had only fifteen letters – she directed him back out on to the road and to the door between her house and the next.

A staircase, steep enough to leave him short of breath very quickly, ended at a tiny landing. He knocked on the single door which was opened by a young woman of such obvious charms that his mind began to race . . . He pulled his thoughts together. 'Señorita Oakley?'

'Yes. What do you want?' she answered in poor Spanish.

He introduced himself in English, explained he'd like to ask her a few questions.

'Why?'

'You have heard that Señor Vickers unfortunately died?'

'I read about it in the Majorcan *Daily Bulletin*. I was really shocked . . .'

'It has now been confirmed that he did not die in an accident, he was killed.'

'God Almighty!'

A man appeared, to stand immediately behind her. 'What's the trouble?' he asked in Castilian.

'He's a policeman.'

'So why's a split come here?'

'He says Keith was murdered!'

The man was sufficiently tall that Alvarez could study his face above her shoulder. Physical features were more often than not an unreliable guide to character, but his named him a thug. A possibility supported by his use of the word 'split'. 'Your name is?'

'What's it to you?'

'I like to know who I'm talking to.'

'Tell him,' she said. There was no response. 'He's Julio Cobos.'

'Thank you, señorita. Perhaps I might now enter and explain more precisely why I'm here?' Without waiting, he stepped inside. The room was obviously furnished for letting – the two easy chairs did not match and their covers were badly worn, four uncomfortable rush-seated chairs were set around a small table, the tiled floor was uncarpeted, there were no curtains, one of the wall lights lacked its cover, several cracks crossed the hanging ceiling, a system of building now seldom used, and the walls needed repainting. As if conditioned by the surroundings, no attempt had been made to clean or dust the room and the remains of what appeared to be more than one meal were on the table.

'All right, so what is it you want?' Cobos demanded.

'As I am investigating the murder of Señor Vickers, I need to speak to anyone who may be able to help me with my inquiries. Señorita Oakley can perhaps do so.'

'She can't.'

'I will be the judge.'

'Get lost.'

'Please, Julio,' she said nervously.

'If he thinks he can come in here and order us around, he'll bloody soon learn different.'

She looked at Alvarez, appealing for his sympathetic understanding.

'Shall we sit, señorita?' he asked.

She crossed to the nearer easy chair, he sat on the other. Cobos remained standing, body slightly hunched, emanating hostility.

'Señorita,' Alvarez said, 'I am afraid you may find some of my questions slightly distressing . . .'

'Then don't ask 'em,' Cobos said violently.

She reached out and was just able to touch his arm in a pacifying gesture.

It failed to pacify. 'Who cares if the bastard was murdered?'

'You mustn't talk like that,' she said, a note of desperation in her voice.

'Stop being such a stupid bitch.'

'Talk again in those terms,' Alvarez said, 'and I'll have you in jail.'

'On what charge?'

'I'll think of one.'

She said: 'Love, why not go out and leave us? Please.'

Cobos hesitated, then crossed to the outside door. He

159

turned. 'You try anything . . .' He went out, slammed the door shut behind him.

'He . . . he has a bit of a temper,' she said. 'And he's so jealous.'

'Of whom?'

'Keith,' she answered, surprised he needed to ask. 'I mean, Keith had everything and he doesn't really have anything. And that made him feel angry. Like when I went back one day and he accused me of trying to get friendly with Keith again, but that's not why I went there and anyway, Keith was away.'

Rosa's memory of that visit named Emma a liar. Lying to protect Cobos or herself from the truth? 'Señorita, during the time you were at Ca'n Mortice, did you ever meet Señora Vickers?'

'Of course not.'

'Would you have recognized her?'

'I came across a photograph one day and asked Keith who the woman was and he told me. He was a bit drunk and was terribly rude about her. He hated her.'

'Did he ever suggest what he thought her feelings were for him?'

'No. But he didn't need to, did he?'

'I suppose not. I understand he had a quick temper?'

'It was like Julio's. Say something he didn't like to hear and he blew his top.'

'So he probably upset a lot of people?'

'Must have done.'

'Do you think he was afraid of anyone in particular?'

'I never heard him say so. Look, I lived with him, but I didn't know that much about him. He kind of built a wall about himself.'

'But you'd probably have gathered if he'd reason to fear someone, wouldn't you?'

'I suppose so,' she answered uncertainly.

'Why did your relationship end?'

She moved uneasily in the chair, which briefly creaked. 'Does that matter?'

'It might do.'

'I don't see how.'

'If it doesn't, I'll forget everything you tell me . . . Was it because the señor discovered you were seeing Julio?'

'How did you know that?' Her voice was high. 'Rosa told you, didn't she?'

'She never mentioned Julio to me.'

'Then how did you know?'

'I didn't, but it seemed a possibility.'

She stared into the past with unfocused eyes. 'It was like living in a palace. Maybe he wasn't half the man he thought he was, but I knew how to make him happy and he kept telling me I was special. I was sure he'd get a divorce and marry me. Then one day I met Julio . . . You know how it goes.'

Offered the wealth of age or the fire of youth, she had tried to enjoy both. 'How did you become friendly with Julio?'

'Keith was returning to England for a fortnight – he was away longer – and wanted me to go with him, only I caught a tummy bug and couldn't move. Two, three days after he'd left, I was better and so bored I went to the big disco in Palma and met Julio.'

'How did Señor Vickers learn about this?'

'Someone must have told him I'd been away from the house every day – I expect it was Rosa since she always disliked me, though I can't think why – and he could be so bloody cunning, he tricked me into admitting I was seeing another bloke. I swore there was nothing going on, which there wasn't . . .' She looked at him. He nodded, as if accepting her denial. 'But he still threw me out.'

Because he was convinced she was lying or because he had become bored with her? How full a life did one need to lead to become bored with a young woman so physically attractive she could make an anchorite rush out from his seclusion . . . ?

'And do you know when he told me to clear out? As soon as we got back from the funeral of the gardener's daughter who'd died from appendicitis, which he'd made me go to with him. I'd told him I hated funerals and that's why he did it like that. He . . . I know he's dead, but he was a really nasty person. He didn't give a damn about the daughter dying, he just went to the funeral to be seen to be doing the right thing, like a gentleman. Gentleman? He walked on his knees in the gutter.'

'You said that when you returned to Ca'n Mortice, Julio thought it was because you were trying to persuade Señor Vickers to have you back . . .'

'I kept telling Julio all I'd wanted was to ask if anyone had found the ring I'd lost, but he gets so jealous you've only to mention the name . . . You saw him just now.'

'Did he believe you?'

'In the end.'

He stood. 'Thank you for your help . . . Señorita, there is a fact you should remember. A person who becomes easily very jealous can be dangerous. I have known women to be in hospital because their men were so jealous.'

'He wouldn't do anything like that.'

'I am glad . . . There is just one more thing. Can you tell me where Julio was on the evening of the twenty-second?'

'Why are you asking? Is that when Keith died?'

'Yes.'

'God! You surely can't think . . . He was here, with me. We stayed in all evening and watched the television.'

'What day of the week was the twenty-second?'

She stared at him, her expression strained.

'You cannot place the evening, yet are certain the two of you were together, here?'

'Yes,' she answered with nervous defiance.

He said goodbye and left. Cobos, a very jealous man, had suspected Emma had tried to persuade Vickers to have her back. A setting for violence. But the murder had been arranged to make it seem an accidental death – was Cobos capable of such subtlety?

CHAPTER 23

Palma had promised to provide the information as soon as possible, which Alvarez translated as tomorrow at the earliest. He settled back in the chair and wondered whether life really was permanent sunshine for the truly rich while they lived? It was said that money couldn't buy happiness, but he'd always reckoned that that had been thought up by the rich to keep the poor content with their impoverished lot.

The phone rang.

'Have you carried out your orders and apologized to Señor Lovell?' Salas demanded.

'Yes, señor.'

'Did he suggest whether he is sufficiently generously minded to overlook the consequences of your crass stupidity?'

'Not exactly.'

'Then what did he say?'

'Very little, really.'

'Being an astute man, he no doubt realizes that the less said to you, the smaller the chance of confusion. Did you return the passport?'

'Yes, señor.'

'You are finally satisfied that a gentleman in his position is hardly likely to have the slightest connection with the murder?'

'He still refused to answer the question, what was the row with Señor Vickers about?'

'You asked him yet again? There are times when as conversant as I am with your unaccountable and irrational behaviour, you still manage to surprise me ... Can you explain why, if you consider the question to be of such importance, you returned the passport despite receiving no answer?'

'I judged that that was what you wanted me to do.'

'Did I specifically say so?'

'Not in so many words, perhaps . . .'

'Then the judgement was solely yours.'

'But you did say . . .'

'Despite the fact that Señor Lovell is an important member of the British government, you still find it feasible to regard him as a suspect?'

'If he's innocent, why does he continue to refuse to answer a simple question? It has to be obvious how important the answer could be.'

'No doubt you have managed to confuse him to the point where he has little or no idea what it is he's really being asked. Is there one single fact which points to his being the murderer?'

'I suppose not.'

'Which, perhaps, is why you continue to suspect him? . . . Have you even considered the possibility that the murderer is someone else?'

'Of course, señor.'

'Have you pursued such a possibility?'

'I've followed up several leads. This afternoon, I drove to Montagut and questioned Señorita Oakley.'

'Who?'

'She was Señor Vickers's girlfriend before he threw her out, either because she had begun to bore him or he was convinced she was having it off with Julio Cobos . . .'

'She was doing what with him?'

'Having sexual intercourse.'

'Must you always revel in unnecessary and salacious details?'

'But those facts are important.'

'In what way?'

'Cobos was very jealous of Señor Vickers. That may sound odd because normally one would expect things to be the other way round . . .'

'I do not have all evening in which to try to understand.'

'I'm reasonably sure Cobos is an ex-con . . .'

'Why are you not certain?'

'I have asked Records to check him out, but they have yet to get back to me. If it turns out he does have a history of violence, then . . .' He became silent.

'Well?'

'On the face of things, he becomes a prime suspect. But I find it difficult to imagine his planning the scene. He'll always act before he thinks. The murderer planned hard and long before he acted.'

'You are now saying you do not consider him to be a prime suspect?'

'As things stand, that's so.'

'Yet a moment ago, you were trying to suggest that it was because he was a prime suspect, you were concerning yourself with salacious details.'

'Those are necessary . . .'

'It has been said that a man can best be judged by the picture he has of himself. I imagine this is something you are careful not to view.' He rang off.

What picture did he have of himself? Alvarez wondered as he replaced the receiver. But even asking the question was to confuse that picture.

Jaime picked up the bottle of brandy, recharged his glass, added a little water and several cubes of ice. 'I've had one hell of a day!'

'Mine's not exactly been a bed of roses,' Alvarez responded.

'If there's anyone thicker than the boss, he could head-butt a concrete wall. Do this, do that, why haven't you done the other, when there isn't time to do anything.'

'The superior chief's never off the phone to me. And I'm having to be polite to an Englishman who makes a lager lout seem good company.'

'Why shouldn't a bloke have a fag now and then, that's what I'd like to know. And when you go into his office, what's he doing? Feet up on the desk, smoking.'

'And I had to drive over to Montagut to talk to the woman even though it was the evening.'

Jaime lowered his glass. 'What was she like?'

'Have you ever thought of love on a tropical beach under a full moon?'

'Can't say I have.'

'She'd outshine the moon.'

'Why do you have all the luck? The only women I get to meet would look out of place even on a beach in Galicia in the middle of winter.'

'She's a fool.'

'What's it matter what her IQ is?'

'She was shacked up with Vickers . . .'

'The bloke who was murdered? Don't tell me. She bumped him off so she can inherit all his money and live like a queen. And you've made your mark? Life's jammy for some.'

'She was keeping him happy, but what does she do? Finds herself a layabout on the quiet because she wants a real man. Vickers finds out and naturally kicks her out of the house. Why are women so stupid?'

Dolores appeared through the bead curtain. She placed her hands on her hips and held her head high; her eyes might well have been flashing fire. 'Women are so stupid because they waste their lives slaving away for men who are incapable of the slightest gratitude since their minds are filled only with thoughts that would bring blushes to their cheeks had they enough decency to blush.'

'Why keep going on like this?' Jaime asked resentfully. 'We were discussing Enrique's latest case.'

'In terms that no decent woman could bear to listen to.'

'Then you won't know what we said.'

'You have drunk so much your tongue is waving in the air.'

'This is my first.'

'Do you think I am both blind and deaf?'

'All right, maybe it is my second.'

More likely, his fourth or fifth, Alvarez thought gloomily. If he went on aggravating Dolores, supper could be a disaster.

He tried to send a telepathic message to Jaime to bow his head and let the storm sweep over him.

'We were talking about Enrique's case. Where's there anything wrong with that?'

'That this woman is a fool not because she betrayed the man who she was living with, but because she allowed him to find that out.'

'It's not . . .'

'Betrayal is amusing, discovery is foolish?'

'I didn't say . . .'

'Had she kept the betrayal a secret, you would admire her. And, of course, lust after her?'

'But it's Enrique who said all that. That sort of thing doesn't worry him, but it does me. Infidelity is unforgivable, and for me it's inconceivable. You know how I think of you.'

'Indeed. Having heard you say that the only women you ever meet would look out of place on a beach even in Galicia in the middle of winter. What could make your thoughts of me plainer?' She swept back into the kitchen amidst a swirl of beads.

'Why does she go for me like that?' Jaime asked plaintively.

'Because you were too busy trying to save yourself at my expense,' Alvarez replied, not trying to hide his bitterness.

Records rang at ten-forty in the morning, minutes after Alvarez had returned from his merienda. Julio Cobos had two convictions, one for a badly planned and stupidly executed theft, one for violence during a domestic argument.

He stared down at the square of paper on which he'd noted the facts. A man who'd hit one woman, breaking her nose and jaw bone, would hardly hesitate to hit another. Emma was living with a man who, because of an overdeveloped sense of jealousy, lack of intelligence, and any sense of morality, would almost always turn to violence to express strong disagreement or frustration. He had warned her of this, but only in very general terms. Did he now return to do so again in far more specific ones? His heart said yes;

experience told him it would be a waste of time. Love, loyalty, self-induced stupidity, would prevent her accepting the truth. He sighed. She was throwing away her future . . .

Yesterday, he had made the snap judgement that Cobos was an unlikely suspect. Should that opinion now be revised? But the two convictions reinforced the suggestion of a man who seldom, if ever, thought ahead. Could he have planned the apparent accident – a bottle of brandy and a used glass in the saloon to give the impression of a man who had drunk too much; the line wrapped around the propeller to make it seem he'd taken the dinghy to try and find the cause of the trouble, had failed to make the painter fast so that when he dived in and returned to the surface after inspecting the propeller, the dinghy had drifted too far away from him to be able to reach it, while he was unable to haul himself back aboard the motor cruiser; the need to weight the dead man's foot so that when the gases formed, the body did not float to the surface (a need that would have been met had a secure knot been tied); the planted bill from Restaurante Monserrat to inculpate Vickers's wife . . . No, what he had just learned was not reason enough to revise that opinion.

He must question Laura Vickers again and challenge her about the reason for that meeting with her husband. Another 'look' at Serra would not come amiss. Was he merely a handsome, weak man, content to be kept by a woman almost old enough to be his mother, or was that a mask?

He looked at his watch. He could drive over to Playa Neuva and expect to return home in good time, except that in the summer tourists in their tens of thousands clogged the roads and journeys could take much longer than they should. He decided to wait until the early evening.

He parked in front of Ca'n Arboles, climbed out of the car, stared at the huge, sweeping bay and remembered it as it had once been, lined with untrodden sand and backed only by farmland and marshes which had been a paradise for migratory birds. Beauty untouched. Yet those had been days when men had worried not about whether they could afford a new car, but whether they and their families would have enough to eat . . .

Francisca opened the front door and led the way through to the patio. Laura lay, face downwards, on a pool mattress. Serra was swimming. As she carefully knotted her bikini top behind her back before raising herself up, Serra stared at Alvarez, his expression a mixture of unease and weak defiance.

'A coincidence?' she asked.

'Señora?'

'It's only a minute ago that I said to Marcos it was time for the evening drink.' She turned her head. 'Isn't that so?'

'Yes,' Serra answered.

'I can assure you, señora, I did not hear you.'

She laughed. 'Suppose you ring the bell which is to the right of the door to call Francisca?'

He crossed back to the doorway, rang the bell.

'Stay there. I've had all the sun I want.'

He sat on one of the patio chairs, haphazardly set around the oblong table, and carefully did not watch her as she stood. Youth might have instant allure, but maturity could possess a special attraction . . .

Francisca stepped out on to the patio.

'The usual for us,' Laura said, as she walked into the shade. 'And the inspector will tell you what he would like.'

'A coñac with just ice, please,' he said.

As Francisca returned into the house, Laura sat. 'What brings you back here?' She saw Serra climb the steps out of the pool. 'I'd stay there if I were you, pet.'

'But . . .'

'Just for the moment.'

Looking as disconcerted as he felt, he retreated into the water.

'Well?' she said.

'It became necessary to force open the safe in Señor Vickers's house; inside were many papers, amongst which were his two wills.'

'Two! Never a man to do things by halves.' She began to

169

run right finger and thumb along the arm of the chair. She tried, and failed, to speak casually. 'What are the main terms of them?'

'His Spanish will covers his property on this island; his Jersey will, all his remaining assets. Subject to one proviso, everything is to be transferred to the Vickers Foundation which will carry out general charitable work.'

'What's the proviso?'

'That sufficient capital is retained and invested to make certain your allowance is paid to you throughout your lifetime.'

She stopped fiddling with the chair arm. 'The Vickers Foundation. How very typical! Hoping to buy a saintly reputation that will bury his earthly one.'

'You are disappointed?'

'It would be hypocritical to say that I haven't been hoping he'd show a glimmer of charity and leave me some solid capital. But at least I can now be certain my allowance will see me to my grave.'

'Which is very fortunate, considering you knew you were threatened with losing it.'

'What's that supposed to mean?' she demanded sharply, and more loudly than intended.

'What is wrong now?' Serra called out from the pool. When she didn't immediately answer, he swam to the steps and, as he climbed them, asked again: 'Is something wrong?'

'Nothing,' she answered.

'I know something is.' He hurried across to where they sat, a trail of dampness on the tiles marking his route. 'What is it?'

'It's just the inspector has said something ridiculous.'

Serra faced Alvarez. 'If you're upsetting her . . .' He tried to sound threatening.

'Yes?' Alvarez asked.

'I'll . . . I'll . . .'

'Why not sit down.'

Francisca returned and, giving no impression of being able to sense the air of tension, placed three glasses and a bowl

170

of crisps on the table. She left. After further hesitation, Serra sat.

Laura passed a glass to Alvarez, another to Serra, picked up the remaining one and drank. 'Just exactly what is it you are suggesting?' She faced Alvarez as, not looking at what she was doing, she put her glass down on the table.

'Señor Vickers had told you he was stopping your allowance.'

'Rubbish. He couldn't do that because I'd made him draw up a legally binding contract, knowing what a twisted bastard he was.'

'But you said –' Serra began.

'I said nothing,' she snapped.

'Was the contract drawn up by a lawyer paid by him?' Alvarez asked.

'Of course. If he wanted me out of the way and quiet, he paid.'

'It seems the lawyer concerned made certain the contract was flawed so that it could be held to be invalid at a later date.'

'He swore it was watertight.'

'He was either incompetent or lying.'

'But he was in one of the busiest London firms . . . You're talking a load of balls.'

'Señora, also in the safe were two letters from a solicitor who, I would imagine, works for a different firm, which make clear Señor Vickers was determined to break the contract under which your allowance was guaranteed; in the second one, the lawyer states that proceedings can start as soon as he is advised they should be. You knew that that was what your husband intended.'

'Of course I didn't.'

'When he met you that once after the separation, it was to tell you face to face what he intended, wasn't it, because he was the kind of man who gained pleasure from another's misfortune?'

'He never mentioned anything of the sort,' she said shrilly.

'And if he had, I'd have told him that if he tried anything, I'd drag him through the courts.'

'Would that have worried him? I do not know what are a wife's rights to financial support under British law, but when money can be transferred around the world at the touch of a button and a man lives in a different country from where his wealth is, it can virtually be impossible to enforce legally based financial obligations.'

'His house is worth a fortune. I could have gone to law here.'

'Where were you married?'

'In England.'

'And you both retained your British nationality?'

'Of course we did.'

'Then no court in Spain would have ruled in the matter.'

'She could have –' Serra began.

'Shut up,' she snapped.

He looked so dismayed that she reached across the table, briefly to rest her fingers on his arm. 'Pet, just leave this to me. You can't be expected to understand.'

'But I –'

'Was just trying to help. You'll help me most by listening and not talking. All right?'

After a moment, he nodded.

She spoke once more to Alvarez. 'You could be right as easily as wrong. But when all's said and done, it doesn't matter now.'

'It matters, señora, because Señor Vickers was murdered and therefore I have to uncover the motive.'

'Surely to God you're not suggesting I could have one?'

'It is certain that you did.'

'That's ridiculous!'

'Señora, do you have a private income?'

'You think I'd have stayed with that fornicating machine all those years if I had?'

'Then if your husband lived, you were going to lose all financial support; you would no longer be able to live here,

172

in much comfort. Perhaps your present, happy relationship would suffer . . .'

'Marcos would never leave me, whatever happened.' She turned to Serra. 'Tell him you wouldn't desert me just because I didn't have much money; tell him you love me because I'm me, not because of what I give you.'

'Of course I wouldn't,' he answered in Mallorquin, sounding less than convincing.

'Understand?' she demanded.

'Indeed, señora,' Alvarez answered ambiguously.

She drank quickly.

'Where did you meet your husband when he told you he was going to stop your allowance?'

'Are you deaf? He never told me that.'

'Was it at Restaurante Monserrat?'

She drained her glass, put it heavily down on the table. 'Why don't you just clear off?'

'Very soon, I will. Where were you on the evening of Thursday, the twenty-second of last month?'

'Here.'

'You can remember that evening sufficiently well to be certain?'

'Yes.'

He spoke to Serra. 'Where were you then?'

'With her,' Serra answered sullenly.

'And you can be equally certain you can remember that particular evening?'

'Yes.'

'How?'

'What d'you mean?'

'How can you be so sure? What happened to fix that evening so firmly in your mind that almost two weeks later you can pick it out from all the others?'

Serra looked hopelessly at Laura; she said to Alvarez with bitter crudeness: 'Bugger off, will you.'

The English often lacked any sense of finesse, he decided as he stood. 'Señora, is there anyone who might be able to corroborate the fact that you were both here on that Thursday?'

173

'Francisca.' Her tone was calmer. 'I'll tell her to come out here,' she said as she stood.

'Thank you, but I would prefer to ask her before you suggest what her answer should be.'

'You're a real bastard!'

She was, he thought, a woman of considerable emotional passion – and, to judge from Serra's presence, physical passion as well.

Francisca was chopping up onions and as he entered the kitchen, she put down the knife. 'Were you here all evening on the twenty-second of last month?' he asked.

'How would I know?'

'You can't specifically remember that evening?'

'Of course I can't.'

'Thank you.'

'I don't understand.'

'I am certain the señorita will explain.'

As he drove down the hill, he judged Laura to be quite capable of planning her husband's death in order to preserve her life of comfort and the illusion of Serra's love. Serra had the physical strength to deliver the fatal blow, but would he have had the mental strength? Would Vickers have willingly taken the two of them aboard *Valhalla*? Was her hatred so extreme as to make certain the horn was thrust into the unconscious man's stomach?

CHAPTER 24

'A fresh coca for you,' Dolores said, as she placed the plate on the kitchen table in front of Alvarez. 'I bought it earlier from the bakery run by Marta's cousin . . . You can tell me what it's like. It's the first thing I've bought there for many months.'

He stirred sugar into the hot chocolate. 'You've always said it's the best bakery in the village.'

'It is. But they sold me a barra that I found was stale when I returned here. I went back and complained, but the chit of a girl behind the counter had the impudence to suggest I'd bought it the day before, not eaten it, and was trying to get a fresh one free. I told Marta what I thought of that and there was a bit of an argument.'

More probably, a heated row, he thought.

'But we met by chance the other day at Susana's and she explained to someone else how, to avoid paying tens of thousand of pesetas to the government in social taxes, she has to employ girls who are just out of school and don't know anything, and then get rid of them just as they're learning. It was obvious she was really explaining and apologizing to me.'

He was grateful she was able to make that assumption; Marta's coca was as light as a fairy's footstep.

'I have to go out to do more shopping. Is there anything you want?'

'No, thanks.'

'Then I'm off.' She left.

He dunked a slice of coca in the hot chocolate and ate. He was sure that much cleverer men than he had pondered the paradox of women's behaviour; a thousand to one, none had come to any valid conclusion. Until today, Dolores had been behaving as if she'd been drinking vinegar; now, Marqués de Riscal. If only the trigger of change could be identified, how much more peaceful life would be . . . He ate a second slice of dunked coca. Perhaps the true paradox was woman. As had been said, If a hen crows, do not presume that a cockerel will lay eggs.

He looked at the clock and noted that he should have been in the office some considerable time before. It was of small moment. Strict watch-keeping was for those who lacked the wit to understand that to rush life was to waste it.

He sat at his desk, stared at the day's mail and wondered if any of it was of sufficient importance to be opened and read. The phone rang.

'Inspector Alvarez . . . Gregorio Obrador here. You sent us a load of papers and files to look through . . . Señor Vickers was a very wealthy man and all his assets are carefully recorded with a running balance of capital appreciation – I can tell you there are a great number of people would like to be as astute an investor as he was! He had current and deposit accounts with several banks and all are in very healthy credit. He kept detailed accounts of personal and household expenditure and these show his cost of living to have been high, but not as high as his total income.'

'Nothing of real interest, then?'

'Depends what you call interesting. What exactly did you expect us to uncover?'

'I don't really know.'

'That helps,' Obrador said dryly.

'Well, anything which might have suggested he had financial problems or if there was a large discrepancy for which you couldn't find an explanation.'

'The only true discrepancy is that his tax returns didn't match his income, but since his capital was abroad and he was able to bring much of what money he needed into the country with plastic, that's normal. I assume it's not under-declaration of income you're after?'

'I leave that sort of thing to the tax hyenas.'

176

'Quite right. Absolutely no point in making their job easier . . . As to financial problems, when you're as wealthy as he, the only one is what next to buy.'

'That's one problem I'd welcome.'

'You're not on your own! . . . I don't know if this can be of any interest, but there is a slight anomaly we noted. At one point, and one only, the records aren't specific.'

'Can you expand that?'

'Sure. In his capital accounts, he listed the purchase of two hundred and fifty thousand pounds' worth of shares in a property company which is identified only by the initials HMPL Limited. We cross-checked and there's no corresponding record of this purchase in his list of shares. We referred back to the bank statements and there is a debit of two hundred and fifty thousand pounds, drawn on one of the Jersey banks, and the only reference is the usual one of the cheque's number. We then went through the used cheque books of that bank and found the stub, but the payee again is only noted as HMPL Limited. This relative anonymity is unique, but I presume, as I suggested earlier, it doesn't really interest you?'

'I don't see how it can.'

'If you want a guess, he received some inside information and took full advantage of that, but decided to cover his tracks. I've met this before. There was the case of a builder from Barcelona who thought he could come here and make his fortune because all the locals were half asleep. He decided where he'd build all the expensive homes the foreigners would rush to buy because he'd heard the whisper that planning permission would be given . . .'

Alvarez listened to a story that had a happy ending – the builder returned to Barcelona a poorer but wiser man, having learned that Mallorquins might look sleepy, but when peseta notes rustled, they became wide awake.

He thanked Obrador, asked for the papers to be returned, said goodbye. He settled back in the chair. As Salas would almost certainly soon point out, he was not making any progress in the case, but if the murderer had been too clever to be identified, then all the effort in the world would gain nothing . . . Soon, his eyelids became heavy.

The cabo at the duty desk was a bumptious young man. 'Going off duty already, Uncle?'

'Pursuing my investigations,' Alvarez replied.

'All the way to Club Llueso?'

He came to a stop. 'Has anyone ever told you what happened to the cock which crowed too loudly? It was the first to get its neck wrung.'

'Not by you, that's for certain. Your hands would shake too much.'

Alvarez resumed walking. In the past, youth had shown respect towards their elders. He made his way to Club Llueso where the barman filled a container with coffee and slotted this into the machine, then poured a brandy. He put the glass down on the bar. 'You're looking glum enough to have lost a ten-thousand-peseta note.'

Alvarez picked up the glass. 'Have you noticed how rude the young are these days?'

'You're asking me, with two teenagers?'

'When I was a kid, if I was rude to an adult I got a clip around the ear.'

'And say what you like, it did more good than all the talk that goes on today. Mustn't hit a child because it affects its character. Needs affecting most of the time. My youngest, Alejandro, had a friend in the house and they were playing with a computer I bought from a pal who works in one of the banks. I'm watching the telly when in comes the pal and interrupts things to say the VDU's packed up. I ask him what's that and he starts shouting, "The brontosauruses still live!" Cocky little sod!' Coffee began to flow into the cup on the machine and he turned round.

Alvarez lifted the glass and drank.

The barman put a small cup of coffee, into which he'd added a dash of milk, on the counter. 'Anything more?'

Alvarez drained the glass, passed it across. 'You can give me another. Did you ever find out what a VDU was?'

'Visual display unit. As I said to Alejandro, how was I supposed to know what the letters meant? He started talking about ROM, DOS, COBOL, DAB . . . I told him, forget it, I'm too old for such talk. Why don't they spell these things out?'

'Saves time, I suppose.'

'So what do they do with the time they save? Watch porn on the Internet. The last phone bill was so high that a few years back it would have paid for a year's visit to the house with green shutters. Remember that?'

'No.'

'You're a poor liar. You sneaked in there whenever you had the chance and thought no one was looking.'

Alvarez picked up the cup and saucer, and glass, and went over to a window table. The house with green shutters had ceased to welcome young men several years before because the influx of eager tourists had proved too strong an opposition, but there had been a time when . . . Some memories were best left buried.

He drank some brandy, poured what remained into the coffee. The bartender was right when he suggested that the use of acronyms had become a modern plague, cropping up everywhere, bewildering those of more mature years. Had they been invented by the young to make the old feel stupid? People writing diaries had often used initials, but that was to hide the identities of those they were criticizing. . . HMPL. Two hundred and fifty thousand pounds to buy shares in a company that was identified only by those initials, whereas every other investment was carefully logged. A bitter row overheard by two independent witnesses, yet denied even when it must have been obvious how absurd such denial was . . .

He drank the coffee, finished the brandy, stood.

'Where's the fire?' the bartender asked.

'In my mind.'

'At your age, it's no good lighting one further down.'

He walked back to the post and climbed the stairs to his office too quickly, arriving in his room breathless and sweating heavily. He switched on the fan, sat, used a handkerchief to mop face and neck. One day, soon, he really must take whatever steps were necessary to get into better physical condition . . .

He phoned the Spanish liaison officer at Interpol and asked for information from the UK on a limited company whose initials were HMPL.

At six-fifteen, he was informed that there was no limited company within the United Kingdom whose registered name had those initials.

He left the office, walked through the hot, airless streets to where his car was parked on the outskirts of the village. He drove out on to the main road, along to the roundabout that so confused tourists it was not unusual to meet a car head-on, and up to Ca Na Atalla.

Dale opened the front door. 'Welcome yet again.'

'You'll be glad to hear, señor, that I need not disturb you. All I should like to have is the address of Señor Lovell if you can give that to me?'

'The simplest thing is to ask him yourself.'

Thinking there was an inferred criticism in that, Alvarez spoke apologetically. 'I'm sorry, but I'm afraid I don't know how to get in touch with him in England which is why I'm bothering you now.'

'You misunderstand me. George is still here. And if I add "unfortunately", you will, I hope, understand I do so solely from his point of view?'

'Of course, señor.'

'A man of tact. As soon as you returned his passport, we tried to book him a flight home, but all the planes were full and he couldn't get one before Thursday afternoon – with their usual competency in forecasting, all the airlines have cut back on flights as the demand for them increases. Naturally, he endeavoured to exert such influence as was seemly, but to no avail. So he's experiencing at first hand the government's doctrine of equality in all things, including suffering . . . You want his address? Ask him for it, but as on your previous visits, I suggest you are as tactful as possible, whatever the provocation, and even if you are personally blamed for the lack of transport.'

'I'm afraid I will have to ask him a question that will almost certainly greatly annoy him.'

'Then it is even more unfortunate for all concerned that his departure has been so delayed . . . Come on through.'

Lovell was sitting in the shade of the patio and reading a book. As Alvarez followed Dale out of the sitting room, he looked up. His expression sharpened.

'A visitor,' Dale said.

'So I observe.'

'He asked me for your address in England, not being aware you were still on the island. I suggested he speak to you directly.'

'Why do you want my address?' Lovell demanded.

'I don't now, señor,' Alvarez answered. 'When I thought you had returned to England, I decided . . .'

'Thanks to you, I missed my flight and have had absurd trouble in booking another. You may rest assured that I shall make a point of expressing my annoyance to the relevant authority.'

'Señor, as you are still here, I have a question to ask.'

Lovell turned to Dale. 'Is the man mental or merely stupid?'

'I am quite certain, the answer is neither. I sense a dogged determination in the face of overwhelming difficulty, rather like that which took Scott too late to the South Pole or Mallory almost to the summit of Mount Everest. But now, since my presence is unnecessary, I'll leave you two together, but not before asking if it's too early for a drink?'

'Yes.'

'I know your feelings on the subject. I was really putting the question to the inspector.'

'He will not be staying.'

'Surely there's no need to rush the man too much? Inspector, would you care for a brandy?'

'Thank you, señor.'

As Dale returned indoors, Lovell shut his book with so

181

forceful a snap that a startled pigeon, which had been pecking around in the grass beyond the pool, flew up and away.

'Señor . . .' Alvarez began.

'I will speak simply, so that there can be no excuse for any misunderstanding. You have repeatedly put to me the same question and have impertinently refused to accept my answer. Initially, I tried to make allowances for your extraordinary behaviour on the grounds that this is not a land where social manners hold an important place, but matters have now gone beyond the point where such allowances can be made. As I intimated earlier, on my return home I shall be making a full report on events and in due course no doubt your superiors will take whatever action they deem necessary. That is all I have to say. You can go now.'

'Señor, I have not asked you this before . . .'

'I am not prepared to continue this conversation.'

'Did Señor Vickers give or lend you two hundred and fifty thousand pounds?'

Lovell stared at Alvarez, mouth slightly open, expression one of consternation. His right hand had been lying along the arm of the chair and he gripped that with a force that strained the flesh over his knuckles.

'And was that sum of money the subject of the row you had with him?' Alvarez waited. A single cicada began to shrill, then several more joined in; further away, dogs barked at each other; the rising and falling whine of a chainsaw came from the direction of the nearest hill.

Dale came out of the sitting room, a small tray in his right hand. He stared at Lovell. 'Are you all right, George?'

'He . . . he says . . .'

'Nothing embarrassingly personal, I trust.' He put the glass down on the table in front of where Alvarez stood. 'Inspector, do sit. It's far too hot to stand on ceremony so I'm sure my cousin will allow a small breach of protocol.'

Alvarez sat.

'George, you still resemble a man who's been shown his obituary and found it rather too accurate. Are you sure you wouldn't like a gin and tonic or a glass of Mr Codorníu's best to help overcome the experience?'

'Perhaps a small gin and tonic,' Lovell replied weakly, as he released his grip on the chair's arm.

'I'll send Beatriz out with it.' Dale returned into the house.

The cicadas continued shrilling and the dogs barking; the chainsaw abruptly stopped.

Lovell made a great effort to speak casually. 'Your question so surprised me, Inspector, that for the moment I was . . . Bewildered perhaps would be the best description.'

The shocked consternation had told Alvarez that he was at last nearing the truth; the change in the other's manner, which for the first time was tinged with politeness, was confirmation of that fact. 'Would you be kind enough to answer the question, señor?'

'Keith Lovell never gave or lent me a penny.'

'Had he done so, would that have placed you in an invidious position since you are in the government?'

'A hypothetical question. I never answer them.'

'Would any financial interest he might have had in commerce or business possibly have conflicted with your position?'

'That is an insolent . . .' He checked the words. 'I hope you will accept my word that there was never any financial dealing between us. Why should you think there had been?'

Beatriz came out on to the patio, handed a glass to Lovell, returned indoors. Lovell drank eagerly.

'It became necessary,' Alvarez said, 'to have Señor Vickers's safe forced open. Since there were a great number of papers inside, these have been examined by an accountant to discover if they can offer any clue as to the motive for murder. He has reported that there is recorded the purchase of two hundred and fifty thousand pounds' worth of shares in a company, but this, contrary to every other entry which is named in full, is identified only by the initials HMPL. There is no British limited company which has those initials; in the list of shares owned, there is no mention of these; bank statements show the sum was drawn on a bank in Jersey but, once again, the company is not fully named. These facts suggest the señor deliberately camouflaged the path of the money, even in his own records, perhaps because the matter was of so sensitive a nature.'

'I don't understand how you can possibly think that this in any way concerns me.'

'Your final initial is L.'

'That . . . that is the only reason?'

'There was your row with the señor . . .'

'Which, as I have said more times than I care to remember, never occurred. I don't suppose you've bothered to realize that my Christian names are George Ryder.' Lovell had abruptly regained his aggressively rude manner. 'Hardly to be confused, I should have thought, with HMPL. Yet you have come here to suggest a large sum of money was given to me in dishonourable circumstances merely because my final initial is L?'

Alvarez was silent.

'I suggest you leave.'

Since there seemed to be nothing more to be gained from continuing the questioning, and his glass was empty, Alvarez left.

CHAPTER 25

Alvarez reached across for the bottle of brandy and refilled his glass. He added four cubes of ice, swilled them around by wiggling the glass, drank.

'I've met statues more talkative than you,' Jaime complained.

'I've been thinking.'

'Why?'

'In a moment of inspiration I may have discovered how to wipe the sneer off someone's face.'

'Whose?'

'An English politician who thinks all us islanders are primitives.'

'Kick him in the goolies.'

'Thereby showing him he's right?'

'How's that? Sometimes I don't begin to understand you.'

'Then we should remain firm friends . . . If you wanted to hide something, would you do it under Dolores's name?'

Jaime looked at the bead curtain. He lowered his voice. 'Not flaming likely. I can't hide anything from her.'

As usual, he'd got the wrong end of the stick, Alvarez thought . . . Because of its nature, Vickers had decided he should conceal the transaction even if the possibility of exposure was very remote – in these circumstances, wouldn't the use of the wife's initials have seemed sufficient camouflage?

Dolores stepped through the bead curtain. 'Are you ready to eat?'

Jaime had been about to pour himself another drink; he hastily withdrew his hand. 'Sure.'

'I've cooked merluza a la vasca.'

That news drove from Alvarez's mind any further thoughts on the Vickers case.

To work through official channels would take a long time, so Alvarez had resorted to unofficial ones. He had rung England direct and spoken to a detective constable who had called him 'sir' and promised the information as soon as possible. Just as 'inspector' was a rank of different importance in the two countries, so 'as soon as possible' had different meanings. He was astonished how quickly the DC rang back to tell him that Mrs Lovell's Christian names were Helen Mary Phyllis.

Having thanked the caller and promised him many brandies if ever he came to Llueso, he replaced the phone. He checked the time. Lovell was returning to England that afternoon, which meant he'd be leaving soon because the drive to the airport would take just under the hour, if traffic were not heavy, and he would have to check in one or two hours before departure, depending on whether his flight was schedule or charter. So to make certain of being able to question him before he left meant doing so right away – which must result in a very late, perhaps even a ruined, lunch. There was no necessity to question Lovell before he returned to England; facts were facts. But after all the verbal humiliations he'd suffered at the other's hands, it would be asking for far more Christian charity than he was prepared to offer not to seize the opportunity of forcing an admission . . .

Beatriz said the family was having an early lunch because the visitor – thank God! – was leaving the house at three o'clock. When he replied that he must speak to Señor Lovell immediately, she told him the family was on the patio.

Dale and Geraldine had finished their strawberries; Lovell, who sat at the centre of the table between them, still had three left on his plate.

Dale said, a touch of annoyance in his voice: 'I won't go so far as to say that for once you are unwelcome, Inspector, but as you can see, we are still eating.'

'I assure you I would not have come here at such a time unless it were necessary.'

'Necessity being the mother of intervention?'

'Esme!' Geraldine said.

'The words came from the Pitt of my stomach.'

Alvarez turned to Lovell. 'Señor, please forgive this untimely interruption; as I have just said, I would not have come here unless it was essential I did. Would you be so very kind as to answer a question?' Alvarez accepted that there was hypocrisy in his over-polite manner, but there were times when hypocrisy was a positive pleasure.

Lovell halved a large strawberry with his spoon. 'This has become intolerable.'

Geraldine tried to lessen the rudeness of the curt observation. 'I'm sure the inspector isn't meaning to be difficult.'

'I doubt he understands what he means.'

'George,' Dale said, 'remember the old adage, Never judge by appearances.'

Geraldine stood. 'Inspector, I'm going through to ask Beatriz to make coffee. Would you like some?'

'Or would you rather have a drink?' Dale asked.

'As I have not yet had lunch, señor, I would prefer a small coñac,' Alvarez admitted.

'Then we'll go inside and organize it while you and George sort out the problem.'

Lovell said: 'A problem can only be solved when both have the capacity to solve it.'

'Or the willingness?'

'Come along in and get the inspector his brandy,' Geraldine said sharply.

As they went into the house, Lovell said, each word encased in ice: 'Even making every possible allowance for the fact of being on this island, your behaviour is totally inexcusable.'

'I'm sorry you should think that,' Alvarez answered.

'To ask the same question again and again after you have been answered is either deliberate rudeness or an incontinence of memory.'

'The last time I was here, I told you the papers from Señor Vickers's safe detailed the purchase of shares in a company that was identified only by initials, when the names of all other holdings were given in full, and that there is no company with those initials registered in Britain. I asked if the money was a loan or a gift to you.'

'And if I understood you correctly, a possibility crowned with difficulty, your only reason for the insulting question was, as incredible as this may seem, that both my name and that of the company ended in an L.'

'It seemed there might be significance in the fact since on the morning of the murder there had been a row between you and Señor Vickers.'

Lovell put down his spoon. 'I really think you must be suffering from some degree of mental trouble.'

'Both Rosa and Luisa testify to this.'

'And you continue to prefer to believe them, even though you call me a liar by doing so?'

'Perhaps they and you have different definitions as to what constitutes a row.'

He picked up his spoon and ate half a strawberry.

'What are your wife's initials, señor?'

For several seconds his jaws were still; then he swallowed. 'None of your business.'

'It has to be.'

'I have nothing more to say to you before I leave.'

'You will not be leaving until you answer me.'

'My God! This is unbelievable.'

'I think you should know that the police in England have told me your wife's Christian names are Helen Mary Phyllis. Her initials are the same as those of the company which, in fact, does not exist. A coincidence too far, I think.'

Lovell tried to inject far more force into his, 'Completely ridiculous,' than he succeeded in doing.

'I ask you again, did Señor Vickers lend or give you two hundred and fifty thousand pounds and was this money the cause of the row you had with him?'

'Why can't you understand that there was no row?'

'Since you persist in your denial, will you please give me your passport.'

'What?'

'Your passport.'

Dale came out on to the patio, a balloon glass in his hand.

'The man's a raving idiot,' Lovell said wildly. 'He's demanding my passport again.'

Dale came to a stop. 'Are you quite sure?' He turned to Alvarez. 'You really are asking for his passport again, which will mean he can't fly back home this afternoon? You do realize that in the circumstances this must cause very considerable trouble?'

'Yes, señor.'

'Then I think both George and I need to join you in a drink.' He came forward and handed the glass to Alvarez, returned indoors.

As he lay on his bed, sweating despite the fan, Alvarez came to the unwelcome conclusion that he had been a fool to allow pleasure to come before self-interest. There had been no need to demand Lovell's passport. He could have been left to return to England whilst the investigation was continued to determine whether there was sufficient evidence to ask for his extradition on a charge of murder. But no, Inspector Alvarez had to get his own back! And adding injury to stupidity, he'd arrived home to find the family had decided he wasn't returning for lunch and so had left him almost nothing . . .

The phone rang.

Because life rejoiced in kicking one when one was down, he was certain the call would prove to be for him. He was right.

'Enrique, Enrique,' Dolores called out from downstairs. He sighed.

'Enrique, are you dead?'

'Yes.' He put on shirt and trousers, made his way downstairs and through to the front room. He picked up the receiver.

'Are you insane?' Salas shouted.

'I hope not, señor.'

'Did you confiscate Señor Lovell's passport yet again this afternoon, thereby preventing his leaving the island on the flight on which he was booked?'

'Yes, señor. You see –'

'I see that I made a fatal mistake when I deemed it necessary to allow you to continue at work until I could find a replacement. I should have ordered one of my other inspectors to replace you immediately since however much crime flourished in his absence, that would have been as nothing compared to the present disaster.'

'Señor, I asked the police in England . . .'

'No such request has passed through my office; had it done so, I would have cancelled it immediately.'

'It seemed best to handle the matter direct . . .'

'Then God knows what's happened. Perhaps Scotland Yard has imploded . . . You are suspended as from this moment. Is that perfectly clear?'

'Señor, I had to do something . . .'

'There is only rationality when you do nothing. You will remain suspended until an official hearing into your conduct is convened, following which you will be dismissed from the service.' He rang off.

Verdict and then trial . . . He made his way back upstairs. At least there was one consolation to be gained out of the sorry mess; suspended, his siesta need never end.

CHAPTER 26

'You're back early,' Jaime said, as he entered the dining room and saw Alvarez seated at the table, a bottle of brandy in front of him.

'I'm not back,' Alvarez replied shortly.

'Bright and cheerful too!'

Dolores swept through the bead curtain, a wooden spoon in her right hand. 'Must you be so stupid?' she demanded, glaring at her husband.

'What have I done now?' he asked plaintively.

'You can ask?'

'Of course I can when I come home from work and you go on at me as if I'd been enjoying myself with a puta.'

'If you ever so much as think about doing that,' she hissed, 'I'll take a knife to your particulars.' She scythed the spoon through the air, then returned into the kitchen.

Jaime sat. 'God Almighty! It's like being married to a volcano. Do I need a drink!'

Alvarez pushed the bottle across the table. Jaime brought a glass out of the sideboard, poured himself a very large measure, added water and several ice cubes. 'What the hell's her problem this time?' he asked in a low voice. 'Is one of the kids ill and she's worried it's something really nasty?'

'No.'

'Then what is wrong?'

'I've been suspended from duty.'

'Really? . . . Well, thank God that's all it is.'

There were times when Alvarez found Jaime as thoughtlessly tactless as Dolores so often claimed him to be.

*　　*　　*

191

Ironically, the knowledge that tomorrow was Saturday failed to have its usual uplifting effect because now all his days were non-working days. It seemed, Alvarez morosely concluded, that one had to suffer before one could appreciate a state of non-suffering.

Dolores looked through the bead curtain. 'You can lay the table.'

'Me?'

'You've nothing else to do.' She withdrew her head.

He might have concluded there was very little chance of obtaining other work, but it was rapidly becoming obvious that he'd have to find something, even if it was only cleaning dishes in a restaurant. If he didn't, Dolores would soon expect him to do all the housework . . .

He laid the table.

Juan rushed in and wanted to know how long the meal would be, rushed out again. Isabel walked in and asked where her mother was and it seemed clear from the gleam in her dark-brown eyes, so like Dolores's, that she had something exciting to say.

He sat at the table, brought bottle and a glass out of the sideboard, and poured himself a drink, then realized there was no ice. Was Dolores in the right kind of mood for him to go through to the kitchen to get some, or would such action provoke her into barbed and bitter comments about men who swilled themselves silly?

Isabel returned to the dining room and was crossing to the stairs when he checked her. 'Would you like to do something for me?'

'No.'

'A nice little girl would say, yes, of course.'

'I'm not a little girl.'

'I apologize. You're a nice big girl now. So will you go into the kitchen and get some ice for me?'

'Why don't you do that?'

He reached into his trouser pocket and brought out several coins from which he selected a fifty-peseta piece which he put on the table.

She looked at it.

He added a second one.

She came forward and picked up the two coins, went through to the kitchen.

He heard Dolores say: 'I suppose that's your uncle drinking again?'

Again? He hadn't yet started.

As Isabel returned with the ice bucket, Jaime came through from the front room. 'Gawd, it's like a furnace today!' He sat. 'I must say it's all right for some, sitting down, doing nothing.'

'Nothing? I've had to lay the table.'

'So where's my glass?'

'In the sideboard.'

'I suppose it's too much effort to get it out for me?' Jaime waited, then leaned over to get himself a glass.

Let him remain out of work, Alvarez thought, and he'd become a dogsbody; even Isabel and Juan would start ordering him about. Retirement, previously a treasured goal, was suddenly a curse . . .

Dolores looked into the room. 'Would someone come and carry things?' She withdrew.

'She's calling for you,' Jaime said.

'Why not for you?'

'When she knows I've been working hard all morning?'

'She's always said she doesn't believe in miracles.'

'Bloody funny!'

Dolores came through the bead curtain, an earthenware dish in each hand. 'When there are two deaf men, it's quicker to do things oneself.' She set the dishes on the table, returned to the kitchen.

'You've put her in a right old mood!' Jaime said.

'That's right, blame me. It's a good job I've broad shoulders.'

'You need 'em, to support that belly!' Jaime was still laughing when Dolores came through with the main dish.

'Where are the children?' she asked.

'Isabel went upstairs and Juan returned outside,' Alvarez answered.

'You didn't think to tell them it was lunchtime?'

'That was obvious.'

'Ayee! What it is to be a woman and have to do everything because a man is capable of doing nothing except raise a glass to his mouth . . . One of you call the children,' she said as she returned to the kitchen.

Jaime and Alvarez looked at each other. Jaime's nerve gave first; he stood. 'If you'd had the sense to tell 'em, I wouldn't be having to do this,' he said resentfully.

As, a couple of minutes later, Dolores began serving, Isabel came down the stairs and Juan in from the street. 'Have you washed your hands?' Dolores asked.

'Yes,' they both answered.

'So where,' she asked as she looked across the table at Juan, 'did you wash yours as you were outside?'

'At Benito's so as they'd be clean when I came in to eat.'

'Clearly neither your father nor your uncle has explained to you that a lie will not be believed if it is obviously utterly ridiculous.'

Juan smirked.

Dolores sat. 'Isabel tells me Teresa Agustín has gone into hospital with appendicitis.' She ate. 'Who'd have thought that of a family who've always put on airs and made out they're so well-connected!'

'You can still get appendicitis if you're first cousin to the King,' Jaime said.

'Must you be so stupid?'

'That's true.'

'At least that makes what you said unusual, if ridiculous.'

'I just don't know. You're supposed to be my wife . . .'

'Supposed?'

'What I mean is, you're my wife yet you're always going on at me.'

'If you talked less, there'd be more sense spoken.' She ate another mouthful. 'I can remember Eulalia, Teresa's aunt, boasting her family were descended from the Count de Almansa. But what she didn't add was that her great-grandfather sharpened knives for a living. If the family hadn't owned that property along the shore, her husband would be sharpening knives for a living today . . . They've a big house in the village, right enough, and part of the family lives in a mansion in Palma, but that doesn't make them a whit better than the rest of us. And now Teresa has appendicitis! Well, I never! They always say that those who try to climb the highest seldom look where they're treading.'

Jaime looked inquiringly at Alvarez, who shrugged his shoulders.

For most of the meal, she continued to speak about Teresa and the Agustín family and when the children had cleared the table and left to play with friends, Jaime was constrained to say: 'Why go on and on about these people?'

'I am doing no such thing.'

'Ask Enrique.'

'I know better what I have been saying than either of you two whose minds have become befuddled.'

'Befuddled, hell! All you've said throughout the meal is how her family's walked around with their noses pointing to the sky. How does appendicitis have anything to do with that?'

'You imagine they can call themselves so grand now?'

'Why not?'

'For you, no doubt, there would be no sense of shame. Indeed, you could forget all about it because, being a man, it is a matter of no importance.'

'What wouldn't be important?'

'Fathering a little bastard.'

'Who's talking about that?'

'As usual, you have not been listening. I should not be astonished. By the end of the meal, you have drunk so much you would not hear the Last Trump.'

'I heard everything you've just said and it doesn't make sense.'

'In future,' she said with sweet venom, 'I will try to remember that when I speak to you, I must do so very simply.'

Jaime expressed himself in field-Mallorquin, then stood and stamped his way to the stairs and up them.

Alvarez said: 'I'm with Jaime. I can't see what appendicitis has to do with a family taking on airs. And where's there any connection between that and producing a child?'

'When I was young, girls made certain they behaved honourably. Sadly, sometimes there was one who had the misfortune to like a man too much and he took advantage of her innocence and later her stupidity showed in her belly. When her time was near, she went away, perhaps to relatives in another province. The family said she had appendicitis. The child was given to adoption and the girl returned to the family with her appendix gone. Everyone knew, no one said. That was how things were done when there was still honour. Now, a girl will parade her little bastard along the street in a pram. We live in sad, sad times.'

'But not for the baby, perhaps? Surely it's better off with its mother?'

'Trust a man to try to excuse his iniquities.' She sniffed loudly. 'I need a short rest – which is all I can allow myself because I must soon once more slave for men who have to ask what "appreciation" means.' She crossed to the stairs.

'What happened when a woman really did have appendicitis?'

She came to a stop. 'Naturally, she made certain all her friends visited the hospital and saw she was not in the maternity ward.'

'Do you think Teresa really didn't have appendicitis?'

'Have I been asked to the hospital?'

'Were you ever likely to be? You aren't a close friend of the family.'

'How can you judge?'

'From the way you've been talking about them.'

'Men understand nothing.' She went up the stairs to disappear from sight.

After a moment, he followed her.

He was drifting off to sleep when into his mind floated the memory of his questioning Emma. At the time, he'd decided he'd learned nothing of any consequence. But might she not have unknowingly told him something of the greatest importance? Old habits died hard, especially for those with narrow minds . . .

CHAPTER 27

Llueso had become a minor artistic centre and there were several galleries. For those who liked to draw or paint reality, within a few kilometres there was scenery dramatic enough for heroic, or serene enough for halcyon, pictures, while for those who preferred abstract subjects, there were innumerable bars.

Alvarez entered Galería Ortiz to come face to face with the statue of a nude woman with exaggerated and detailed proportions.

'Daydreaming of yourself as another Pygmalion?' Gual asked, as he came up to where Alvarez stood. 'You can take her home and breathe life into her for four hundred thousand pesetas.'

'If I took that home, Dolores would throw the both of us out of the house.'

'The artist's works are popular with Belgians. They seem to like their woman large and very obvious . . . If you're not buying, what do you want?'

'Some information.'

'On art? You surprise me.'

'If I describe a painting, can you tell me anything about it?'

'Describe and I'll answer you.'

'There's a large animal, bull or cow, it's impossible to be certain because of angles, and on it is a woman who's wearing very little and has a ring of flowers around her neck; they're heading towards the sea which is as calm as a millpond. Behind her are several other women, even more scantily dressed, and in the sea is a bloke with a luxurious black beard who's holding up a trident . . . Does it ring any bells?'

'Without a doubt, the subject is Europa.'

'Who painted it?'

'There's not one painting, but very many by diverse paint-ers; off the cuff, I can name Titian, Veronese and Albini. There's no accounting how many lesser masters and down-right incompetents have tried their hand. It's a popular subject because in a sense Europa was raped and sex with a sting has always helped sales, especially amongst those who like to enjoy a whiff of pornography in the name of art.'

'What more can you tell me about it?'

'Don't you know the myth?'

'No.'

'Too busy trying to cope with the problems of the modern world to listen to those of the ancient one? . . . Jupiter, the Roman father of heaven and often identified with Zeus, was married to Juno, but spent much of his time enjoying himself with other goddesses and sometimes even mortal women – the ancients allowed their gods a much happier life than we do. Juno was jealous, so Jupiter had to be careful and often courted in disguise. He saw Europa and lusted, changed himself into a bull and approached her so peacefully and artfully that she decked him out with flowers and finally hopped on to his back. At which point he told her not to be afraid because he was really Jupiter and swam in the sea calmed by Poseidon – the god with the trident – finally to arrive at Crete where he resumed a more orthodox form, thereby avoiding any hint of bestiality. In her honour, he gave the name of Europe to where he'd had his fun . . . A far more entertaining history of our continent than traditional textbooks offer. Have I told you enough to help?'

'You have.'

'You don't want to know the names of her sons or what happened after Jupiter started grazing in other fields?'

'I don't think so, thanks.'

'Are you going to tell me what this is all about?'

'No.'

'Then I'm sorry I've been so helpful.'

*   *   *

200

Alvarez braked the car to a stop, switched off the engine, climbed out on to the sun-baked earth covered with withered grass. He squinted as he stared across at Ana who was picking sweet peppers and, probably because he had just driven from the gallery, remembered a coloured postcard his mother had kept on a shelf above the open fireplace which had pictured peasants in a field, bowed down to their work . . . He heard movements and turned.

'You want something?' Marti asked, as he came to a stop.

'A word with you.'

He turned and walked towards the house; Alvarez followed. Ana straightened up and watched, her face hardly visible in the strong shadow of the straw hat, then dropped the basket in her hand and took a step towards them.

'Keep picking,' Marti called out roughly.

She returned to her work.

Marti entered the house. 'Wine?'

'If you're offering me some.'

He left the room through the inner doorway. Alvarez sat on one of the uncomfortable chairs. There was something about the scene – though of certainty, not the paintings – that took him back to a day when he'd been waiting for Juana-María to appear together with mother, aunt, or other female relative. A duenna had accompanied every unmarried young woman who hoped to maintain her reputation or could not escape the other's attendance. The young of today looked back on such a time with scorn, but much of the fun of courtship had been in trying to outwit the duenna just long enough to steal a kiss . . .

Marti returned with a bottle and a glass, handed both to Alvarez, sat.

'When I turn up,' Alvarez said, 'most people ask me what I want. It's interesting that you did not.'

There was no response.

'You know why I'm here, don't you?'

'I know nothing.'

'Which makes you a very wise man . . . Have you and Ana ever eaten at Restaurante Monserrat in Runyman?'

'We don't eat in restaurants.'

'I should have started to understand when Rosa told me you liked nothing better than a mug of coffee in the morning, but you'd suddenly stopped drinking it. I ought to have asked myself, why had this happened? Then maybe I would have come up with the answer, it was because you liked it so much.'

Marti abruptly left the room; when he returned, he had a glass in his hand and he crossed to where Alvarez sat, picked up the bottle and filled it with wine.

'You are going to drink? Won't that damn your soul?'

'I like wine as much as you.'

'But you told me you are forbidden to drink it.'

'No longer.'

'Why not?'

'The elders were here yesterday and told me I could not remain in the flock.'

'For what reason?'

'One doesn't question them.'

'But I'll guarantee they told you. It was because you had not burned your paintings, because you had defied them to the extent of painting another, wasn't it?'

'How would I know?'

'And you hadn't burned them because they were Ana's and she wanted to keep them and her wishes were stronger than the elders' orders. And you had not stopped painting because there was one more you had to do; your sanity demanded that. But they couldn't understand that human beauty doesn't necessarily signify lust, even less that your last painting was born out of pain, not pleasure.'

Marti drank.

'When you painted Europa, every brush stroke must have cut like a knife.'

'Shut your bloody mouth!'

'I know what it's like to lose someone one loves. My fiancée was killed by a drunken Frenchman. It happened many, many years ago, but if I met that Frenchman tomorrow I would still want to carve her initials deep in his guts. We are told to forgive our enemies, to turn the other cheek, but one has to be a saint or a coward to do that. You are neither, which is why you killed Vickers.'

'You're full of shit!'

'Carolina was beautiful, but very naive because life here was strict and narrow. Vickers, as do so many wealthy men, believed his money gave him the right to anything, no matter at what cost to anyone else. He lusted after women, the younger, the more insistently; for men like him, there is extra pleasure in destroying innocence. Having met her by chance, no doubt when she was at Ca'n Mortice to speak to you, he pursued her with his wealth and dazzled her so successfully she hid the liaison from you, despite the fact that you had taught her to honour truth.

'Because of her naivety and sense of embarrassment, she did not seek advice on birth control; perhaps she relied on old wives' remedies, whispered at school. Vickers was indifferently careless, seeing her as merely a peasant girl who would sooner or later be paid off with a few pesetas. Inevitably, she became pregnant . . .'

'Shut up!' Marti said violently.

Unseen by them, Ana had been standing just beyond the doorway; she came into the room, crossed to where Marti sat, put her arms around him and pressed him against herself. Tears trickled down her lined, leathered cheeks. 'Why didn't she tell us?' she asked, addressing life, not them. 'We were her parents and nothing else mattered. We would have taken her to see the doctor who would have told us, there would be troubles. Why didn't she tell us?'

Were they responsible because of the severity of their faith? This was the question which had haunted them from the day they'd learned the truth when she'd been rushed into hospital, Alvarez thought sadly. It was the question which had driven Marti to painting Europa which he knew must result in his being thrown out of the sect. Perhaps subconsciously, that was what he wanted. Guilt could sometimes be eased by suffering or self-denial.

Ana released Marti. She hurried through to the next room

and when she returned, had a glass. Alvarez held up the bottle. She emptied it into her glass, returned to stand by her husband.

'From the moment you learned the truth, you determined to murder Vickers,' Alvarez said.

Ana laid her free hand on Marti's shoulder and began to stroke his neck with her forefinger.

'And with your artistic mind, you took your time to plan an artistic murder that would look like an accident. Had you not hated Vickers so deeply that you always avoided him whenever possible and so did not know he had suddenly stopped drinking coñac, had you been more of a seaman and could tie a knot that held, or which way a propeller turned, you would have succeeded.

'When the body floated ashore, murder was certain, but the significance of the horn thrust into the stomach seemed inexplicable. That was until I had reason to remember the painting you had done after being forbidden to paint again and I found out about the myth of Europa. That told me you had gained revenge for the rape – because that was what her unworldly innocence and naivety made it – of your daughter.'

Ana put her free arm around her husband and once more pressed him to herself; some wine slopped over the rim of the glass on to him, but neither of them appeared aware of that fact. 'What . . . what happens?' she asked, her voice twisted by fear.

Alvarez said: 'I have had to determine who might benefit from Vickers's death and in consequence have uncovered motives so mean and sordid that revengeful punishment becomes honourable.'

'What's all that mean?' Marti demanded hoarsely.

'That all I have said so far is pure conjecture. There is no proof that you and Ana had a meal at the restaurant in order to . . .'

'I told you, we've never been near the place.'

'Indeed, and being a man of few words, you've told me very little else. Which has to be to your advantage since a man of many words so often provides his own guilt.'

They stared at him. Ana's expression was one of fearful confusion; Marti's was enigmatic.

'Did your daughter know Vickers?' Alvarez asked.

'Just once she said –' Ana began.

Marti interrupted her. 'She said nothing.'

Alvarez said: 'She didn't name him when she was in hospital?'

'No.'

'Then there can be no certainty he was the father of the unborn child . . . Was your daughter buried or cremated?'

'Cremated. The brothers demanded that because fire is the only element that can cleanse.'

'Then there can be no DNA test on the remains of the foetus. Did you know about the mounted bull's horn in the saloon of the *Valhalla*?'

'Never went inside the boat.'

'Not even when Vickers took the staff for a trip?'

'I didn't go.'

'You once told me how much you dislike the sea, didn't you?'

'Yes.'

'Then you can't know anything about boats?'

'Nothing.'

'But you've always been able to tie a good knot?'

'No.'

'Surely, as a farmer you often have to tie knots that won't come undone, whatever the strains put on them?'

Marti was silent.

'Whoever attached the weight to Vickers's ankle before throwing him overboard probably tied a granny instead of a reef knot. With your experience, you couldn't possibly make a mistake like that, could you, even when under great emotional strain?'

'No.'

'You misunderstood my question?'

'Yes.'

'Where were you on the evening of Thursday, the twenty-second of last month, after you finished work?'

'Here.'

'With Ana?'

'Yes.'

Alvarez spoke to her. 'You can confirm that?'

'I don't understand . . .' she began.

'She confirms it,' Marti said.

'Then it's obviously impossible it could have been you who stood on the rock and attracted Vickers's attention when he had begun to sail out of the cove; that you told him your car had broken down and asked him to sail you to the port; that he agreed and you were aboard the *Valhalla* when it left the cove. And if you weren't aboard, it could not have been you who picked up a metal bar and smashed it down on his head. Any more than it could have been you who – not knowing who had fathered the unborn child – had reason to thrust the bull's horn into his stomach in an act of bizarre revenge.' Alvarez drained his glass. 'In view of all you've just said, you've convinced me it's impossible that my earlier suspicions had any foundation in fact. My accusations were absurd.'

Beatriz opened the front door of Ca Na Atalla. 'You again! You must enjoy coming here.'

'I don't think I can say that,' Alvarez replied.

'The señor and señora are out, but Señor Lovell's still here, worse luck.'

'I don't think he'll be bothering you much longer. Where will I find him?'

'On the patio.'

'Is it all right if I go through?'

'Suit yourself. But if I had the chance, I'd get as far away from him as I could.'

He went through the house to the patio. Lovell laid down the newspaper on the table and, his expression pinched, said: 'I was assured you had been suspended from duty.'

'That is correct, but before returning your passport, I wanted to explain something.'

'There is nothing you can say that will explain or excuse your behaviour or alter by one word the report I shall be making on my return home.'

'I should still like to speak. Señor, would you mind if I sat? It is very hot today.'

There was no reply. Alvarez remained standing. 'I have not come here to try to persuade you to change your opinion.'

'Let me assure you that that is an impossibility.'

'I am here to explain that although I believed I could iden-tify the murderer of Señor Vickers, I now know I was mis-taken. Therefore, evidence concerning other persons must be considered more closely than has been done so far.'

'Having been suspended, presumably you will be consider-ing nothing.'

'But someone will do so.'

'A matter of no concern to me.'

'But it might be. You will remember my telling you Señor Vickers's accounts showed a large sum of money had been spent on shares in a company that did not exist?'

'I also recall your absurd and insulting suggestion that in fact this was money given or lent to me.'

'It was because of your assurance that this was not the case that I did not pursue the matter. But I am sure it will now become necessary to confirm your denial – not, I hasten to add, because your word is to be doubted, but, as you will appreciate, in a major investigation every possibility must be exhaustively examined. This means that, however regrettable, your wife's financial affairs will have to be examined very closely to confirm that the cheque drawn by Señor Vickers did not pass through an account of hers, including any offshore one.'

Lovell stared into space. A dog started barking and this seemed to jerk his attention back to the present. He looked up. 'Would you like to sit, Inspector?'

Alvarez sat.

'Serving one's nation carries a very heavy burden.'

'I am sure that is true, señor.'

'A burden whose weight can be greatly increased by gross misrepresentation. In my country we have a media which loses no opportunity maliciously to attack those in power. Truth is brushed to one side, a small and innocuous detail is presented as a damning and career-threatening allegation, and this must cause great harm even when it is later shown to be utterly baseless. Because of that . . . You are a person of great understanding, are you not, Inspector?'

'I have always tried to be.'

'If he tells the truth, the full truth, I am certain there is not a man alive who would claim he has never once done something which on mature reflection he would prefer not to have done; not because it was wrong, but because it was of a nature that could allow others to come to falsely harmful conclusions . . . I was persuaded into an imprudent investment and found myself in a position which could have led to my being declared bankrupt with the consequence that I would have been forced to leave the government. Keith Vickers lent me the money to help me avoid this. But because the media would have twisted the details into damaging allegations, perhaps even going so far as to hint at bribery, we agreed to keep the loan secret.'

'And the row with Señor Vickers concerned this loan?'

'There was no –' he began, then stopped. 'Yes, it was. As a man of rectitude, I have always found difficulty in accepting that others may not hold to the same high standards. I considered Keith to be a true friend and saw his loan as the act of a selfless and generous person; I swear that at the time it simply did not occur to me for one single moment that there could be any ulterior motive to the giving. But later it became all too clear that my having accepted it, he thought I would, when the time was right, offer him confidential information that would be greatly to his advantage. Naturally, I made it absolutely clear that I would do no such thing.'

'Did he threaten to make the loan public if you continued to refuse?'

'He tried to do so until I pointed out that he had clearly intended it to be a bribe. So while I had made a misjudgement, he had committed a criminal offence.'

'He stopped threatening you?'

'He had no option . . . You will appreciate how these facts could be grossly misinterpreted by the media?'

'Indeed.'

'Then I am sure that, as a man of very great understanding, you will keep the information strictly to yourself?'

'I certainly would if . . .'

'If what?'

'Señor, I have been suspended from duty and so I will have to pass on all the information I have to whoever takes my place. He may well decide to pursue the matter further, not possessing my appreciation of events through having been with the case from the beginning, and this would involve him asking for an investigation in England into the true nature of the loan. He would, of course, suggest there would be confidentiality, but as you will know only too well, one person can keep that promise, two may, three cannot.'

There was a long silence.

Lovell finally said: 'Am I correct in believing you have been suspended solely because of the many complaints I have made concerning your behaviour?'

'That is so.'

'If I were to inform the relevant authorities that I have been suffering from the effects of overwork and my judgement has been greatly disturbed; that on mature reflection, I am sure I have maligned you; that your behaviour has, in truth, at all times been irreproachable, what do you think would be the result?'

'My superior chief would have to reinstate me.'

'And once reinstated . . . ?'

'Naturally, I should be able to observe your request to keep secret facts that I can be certain are of no consequence to the investigation into Señor Vickers's murder, and this even if that is never solved.'

'My cousin was right. One should never judge by appearances. I think, Inspector, it is fortunate for the present government that you are not a member of the opposition.'

Alvarez settled behind the wheel of the Ibiza, started the engine, engaged first and drove round in a tight circle to the entrance gateway; the dirt track was clear and he drew out on to it. Had Lovell, who'd proved himself a liar, been lying or telling the truth when he'd said he'd refused to accede to Vicker's demands for sensitive information? Rosa had mentioned that after Lovell's departure that Thursday morning, Vickers had been smiling despite the anger he had shown earlier – a smile could express satisfaction as well as humour . . .

Corruption was a deadly enemy of any society and needed to be pursued and expunged before, like a cancer, it destroyed the host on which it preyed. So surely, whatever he'd promised Lovell, he should inform the British authorities of the facts? They could determine the truth and decide what action to take . . . But if he were responsible for a detailed investigation into Lovell's affairs, it was probable that the other – a vindictive man – would respond by reversing his evidence and, with added venom, once more accuse Inspector Alvarez of having acted with rude, insolent incompetence throughout the investigation, with the inevitable result . . .

He reached the T-junction and turned on to the macadam-surfaced lane which almost immediately brought him to a 'Stop' sign. And as he braked to a halt, he decided that he was troubling his conscience unnecessarily. Vickers was dead so past corruption had died with him and future corruption fuelled by him was impossible. And if Lovell had acted dishonestly, that would hardly make him unique in the political world, so all corruption would not be eliminated by his downfall. Further, one could be certain he would never take such a risk again . . .

Happy that the course of action advantageous to himself was, in practical terms, the most sensible to pursue, he turned right on to the road and headed home for a welcome drink; or drinks.